“Will you marry me, Cassie?”

She glared at him. “It’s not funny!”

Nick sat down and took her hand. “Look, Cassie, just for now play along. Until Max and Julia sort themselves out, at least.”

Cassie eyed him suspiciously, then sighed. “I suppose so.”

He put a finger under her chin. “In the meantime, would you be surprised to know…I do want to kiss you? Most of the time.” His lips settled on hers. When she made no protest he slid his hands into her hair and held her fast, kissing her with an unexpected tenderness that breached her defenses far more than any masterful display of passion.

CATHERINE GEORGE was born in Wales, and early on developed a passion for reading, which eventually fueled her compulsion to write. Marriage to an engineer led to nine years in Brazil, but on his later travels the education of her son and daughter kept her in the U.K. And instead of constant reading to pass her lonely evenings, she began to write the first of her romantic novels. When not writing and reading she loves to cook, listen to opera, browse in antiques shops and walk the Labrador.

Look out for the fabulous new book in Catherine George's popular Dysarts series. *Sweet Surrender* is on sale early next year in Harlequin Presents®.

Books by Catherine George

HARLEQUIN PRESENTS®

2225—HUSBAND FOR REAL
2244—RESTLESS NIGHTS

Catherine George

FIANCÉ FOR CHRISTMAS

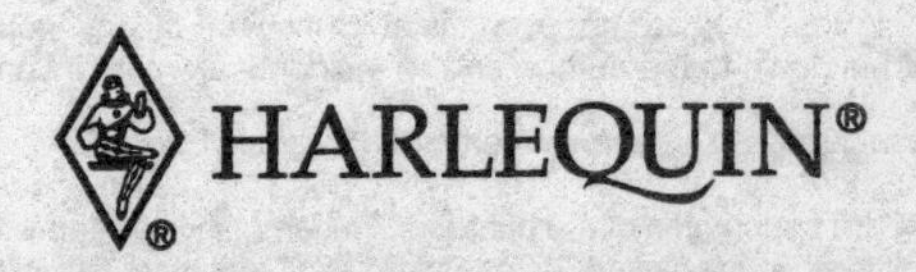

TORONTO • NEW YORK • LONDON
AMSTERDAM • PARIS • SYDNEY • HAMBURG
STOCKHOLM • ATHENS • TOKYO • MILAN • MADRID
PRAGUE • WARSAW • BUDAPEST • AUCKLAND

ISBN 0-373-12293-4

FIANCÉ FOR CHRISTMAS

First North American Publication 2002.

This edition published by arrangement with Harlequin Books S.A.

Visit us at www.eHarlequin.com

Printed in U.S.A.

CHAPTER ONE

CASSIE was good at organisation. And sharing a house was a lot of fun. Most of the time, anyway. But to get the place to herself for once, to entertain a special guest to dinner, had taken only slightly less organisation than the Olympic Games. Now, at last, two of her friends were at that very moment winging their way to a Christmas ski-holiday, and the other two were safely out with their men after swearing a blood oath not to return before the small hours.

Not, of course, that Rupert was certain to stay that long. But he might. In the meantime there were things to be done. Not famed for her cooking skills, Cassie had opted for a visit to the hairdresser instead of attempting the impossible, and lashed out on an extravagant, ready-to-cook meal on the way home. After a swift bath, and twice the usual time spent on her face, she ran down to the large sitting-room to make sure it was immaculate for once. Normally she ate with the others in the kitchen, or from a tray on her knees in front of the television, but tonight, for Rupert, something special was called for. Which meant using the small round table under the window. Cassie eyed it thoughtfully, wondering whether to use her embroidered scarlet cover as a tablecloth, or save it for her bed.

Cassie quickly draped the cover over the table. No male had ever crossed the threshold of her bedroom up to now. Nor been invited to do so. But if by any chance things did progress that far Rupert would hardly take time out to admire the decor. Not, of course, Cassie assured herself, that things would get that far. But with Rupert it just *might* be different.

As eight o'clock loomed closer Cassie stepped into her dévoré velvet dress and turned the heating up to compensate for brief sleeves and a lot more sheer dark stocking on view than usual. No way could she spoil her splendour with a woolly cardigan and opaque tights. She eyed her reflection, searching, wondering if she'd gone too far over the top. She'd fully intended having her fair curly hair straightened and smoothed out, to look more sophisticated. Instead she'd let the young male hairdresser cajole her into a few strategic gilt highlights before he transformed her mop into a mane of extravagant ringlets. Combined with the skimpy burgundy velvet, the effect was vastly different from Cassandra Lovell, efficient administrative assistant, who wore neat suits to her job at the bank, and brushed her hair into a French pleat.

Cassie put tomato and basil soup in a pan over a low flame, placed salmon in watercress sauce ready in the microwave, and arranged baby vegetables ready to steam over tiny potatoes. Everything, she decided, was as ready as it could be. The only thing missing was the guest of honour. When the doorbell rang, ten minutes earlier than expected, Cassie took a quick look in the mirror over the kitchen sink, then hurried into the hall and switched on the light—with no result. She sighed, made a mental note to put electric lightbulbs on the communal shopping list, then opened the door, smiling in welcome.

'Where is she?' demanded the man who pushed past her. Without so much as a glance at her he strode into the sitting-room, his mouth tightening as he eyed the table set for two.

'Very cosy, Julia,' he snarled, and spun round to face the girl who stood glaring at him from the doorway.

'What on earth are you doing here?' demanded Cassie furiously. 'Julia doesn't live here any more.'

If she hadn't been so angry Cassie would have laughed at the blank astonishment on Dominic Seymour's face. He was blue with cold under a deep-dyed tan, his black, collar-length hair dishevelled; he was in dire need of a shave, and fatigue dulled brilliant blue eyes rimmed with lashes so black the eyes appeared set in, Irish fashion, with a sooty finger. He wore a raincoat over a crumpled linen suit totally unsuitable for London in December, and he was shivering.

'Cassandra?' he said, frowning.

'That's me,' she snapped. 'And delighted though I am to see you, of course, I must ask you to go. I'm expecting company.'

'Until I saw you in the light I thought you were Julia. You've grown up, Cassie.'

'Unlike you!' she retorted. '*Still* chasing after my sister? Can't you just let her alone?'

The effect of her words were startling. He closed the space between them and seized Cassie ungently by her bare elbows. 'I wasn't chasing after *Julia*. I'm looking for Alice. Is she in bed?'

Cassie stared at him incredulously. 'Alice? No, of course not. I haven't seen her since I took her out from school for the day three weeks ago—' She stopped, biting her lip, and Nick's hands fell away as he stood back.

'It's all right. I know you see her from time to time,' he said quickly.

'Good,' she said defiantly, and folded her arms across her chest. 'Julia's the one forbidden to see her. Not me. Nor my mother.'

The blue eyes softened for an instant, then blazed again with anxiety. 'But hell, Cassie, if Alice isn't here, where is she?'

'I don't *know*,' she retorted, troubled. 'I thought Max was collecting her today for the Christmas holidays.'

'That was the plan,' he returned grimly. 'I've just got in from Riyadh to find my celebrated brother isn't back from New Guinea.'

Cassie gazed at him in horror. 'But what about Alice? She's eight years old, for heaven's sake. Surely he arranged some emergency plan—'

'He did. Don't panic,' said Nick swiftly. 'The minute I got back I contacted my answering service. There was a message from the school to say some people called Cartwright were taking her home with them.'

'Laura Cartwright's her best friend,' said Cassie in relief. 'If they've got her she's fine.'

'The school gave me their number, but there was no answer. If Alice is with these Cartwright people, surely someone should be there at this time of night?'

'You'd think so certainly,' agreed Cassie, worried, then her eyes flashed. 'Which doesn't explain why you came storming round here. Though I can guess!'

'Alice left this number with my service for emergencies, so I assumed these Cartwright people had brought her here.'

'An address you once knew very well, of course,' snapped Cassie. 'Sorry to disappoint you but *I* took over Julia's share of the house—but never mind all that. Try the Cartwrights' number again.'

Nick raised a hostile eyebrow at her tone, but after a quick look in his diary punched in the Cartwrights' number on his cellphone. With no result. 'I don't like this,' he said grimly.

'Neither do I!'

They stared at each other in worried silence, then Nick heaved a ragged sigh. 'Look, could I have a wash, please? I slept in fits and starts on the flight back. My head's full of cotton wool. Perhaps if I freshen up I can think up something constructive.'

'Of course. Upstairs, first on the right.'

Cassie went into the kitchen to switch off the heat under the soup, trying not to panic. She was fond of young Alice, and could have wrung Max Seymour's neck for not getting home on time to pick his little daughter up for the Christmas holidays. When the front doorbell rang again, dead on time, Cassie sighed despairingly. She'd spent so much time and effort on this one evening, and now all she could think about was Alice. She opened the door in the dark hall and Rupert Ashcroft, resplendent in formal suit, fair hair gleaming under the streetlamp, handed her a large bouquet of flowers.

'Hello, Cassie, these are for you.'

'How lovely, Rupert, thank you. Do come in. Go on into the sitting-room; I'll just put these in water.' When she joined him Rupert was surveying his surroundings with obvious satisfaction, taking in the table set for two with candles and flowers.

'This all looks very inviting, Cassie—' he began as he turned to her, then stopped, staring, transfixed. The Medusa-style ringlets, she thought, resigned, had a lot to answer for. One look at her and men turned to stone.

'Cassie!' said Rupert huskily, coming to life. 'You look sensational!' He moved closer, his smile altering subtly as his eyes roved over her in a way which made her suddenly very conscious of bare arms and generous display of legs.

She smiled warily. 'Actually, I'm afraid I'm a bit behind with dinner—' The rest of her explanation was cut off as Rupert took her in his arms and kissed her with an enthusiasm which hinted that her transformation had ignited him with an appetite for rather more than just dinner.

'I can't believe it,' he said huskily, holding her tightly as Cassie tried to wriggle away. 'Miss Efficient by day and Miss Sexpot at night—'

'Am I intruding?' enquired a voice from the doorway.

If an archangel with a flaming sword had appeared in Cassie's sitting-room her guest could hardly have been less dumbfounded. Rupert let her go so promptly she staggered as the tall, hostile intruder came forward with outstretched hand.

'Dominic Seymour.'

Rupert took the hand reluctantly, muttered his name, and cast an accusing look at Cassie.

'Nick just flew in from the Middle East—he's a civil engineer,' she explained hurriedly, and turned to Nick. 'I provide administrative assistance to the team Rupert works with.'

'Team?' he queried, as though Rupert played for some amateur soccer club.

'I'm an analyst with an investment bank,' said Rupert, bristling.

Cassie gave him a cajoling smile. 'Look, Rupert, sit down and make yourself at home. Help yourself to a drink from the tray over there while I talk to Nick for a moment. He's my sister's brother-in-law,' she added. 'There's a family emergency.'

The information seemed to appease Rupert slightly, and Cassie smiled at him again, then went off to the kitchen with Nick and closed the door behind them.

'Ring the Cartwright number again,' she said urgently.

This time someone answered, but as Cassie listened to the brief, one-sided conversation her heart sank.

Nick's face was haggard as he rang off. 'That was the Cartwrights' teenage son. His parents are out, but he was quite definite that his mother had delivered Alice to Max's place in Chiswick first, before bringing his sister home.'

'Surely Mrs Cartwright wouldn't have left Alice in a deserted house?' said Cassie, getting more worried by the minute.

'I bloody well hope not!' said Nick savagely, and began punching buttons on his phone again. He listened for a few moments, then switched off the phone. 'No response from Max's place,' he said tightly. 'I'm going round there.'

At the thought of Alice, alone and frightened in Max Seymour's house, Cassie's enthusiasm for a cosy dinner for two vanished completely. 'I'll make my excuses to Rupert and come with you.'

'You will not!' he objected. 'I'm Alice's blood relative. I'll do what's necessary.'

'And leave me here, wondering what's happened to her?' retorted Cassie angrily. 'I'm very fond of Alice. I may not be related, but who actually turns up for Sports Day and *exeats* from school, Dominic Seymour? My mother, or me, now Max won't let Julia near Alice. When Daddy and Uncle Nick are on the other side of the world the poor little thing's a bit short of blood relatives when it matters, isn't she?'

They were standing close, her dark eyes spitting flame into the angry blue ones locked with hers.

'Am I intruding?' said a sarcastic voice from the doorway, and both combatants spun round to face Rupert, staring at him blankly.

Cassie pulled herself together. 'Rupert, I'm so sorry about this. The reason Nick is here is Alice, his eight-year-old niece. She's missing, and we're worried to death about her.'

Rupert's face altered dramatically. 'Oh, I say. I'm frightfully sorry. Is there anything I can do?'

'No,' said Nick curtly. 'Thanks anyway. I'm just off to look for her.'

'I'm coming with you,' said Cassie firmly. She looked at Rupert in appeal. 'I hate to do this, but would you mind terribly if we postponed dinner to another time? If—when—we find Alice, she'll need me.'

Rupert Ashcroft controlled an involuntary look of dismay, duly insisted he didn't mind at all under the circumstances, and even managed a smile. 'I'll take myself off, then, Cassie, and look forward to doing this some other time soon. Please ring me and let me know what happens.'

She nodded gratefully, saw him to the door and reached up to kiss his cheek. 'Thanks for being so understanding, Rupert. See you Monday.'

He kissed her mouth very deliberately, ignoring the stony blue eyes watching the procedure, then went off to the gleaming Range Rover parked a little way down the road.

Cassie closed the door and raced past Nick in the hall. 'Give me five minutes to change and I'll be with you.'

'There's absolutely no need for you to come,' he snapped irritably, but Cassie shook her head as she ran upstairs.

'I'm coming, and that's that. If you won't drive me I'll call a cab.'

Cassie heard Nick swear under his breath, but he was still there when she ran down again in jeans and a sweater, her ringlets tied up with a shoelace. She reached for a long dark overcoat from the assortment on the hall pegs, slung her bag over her shoulder and looked at the waiting man impatiently.

'Come *on*, then.'

Nick Seymour's car, like Rupert's, was an all-wheel drive, a fairly new Subaru estate. But, unlike the gleaming Range Rover, it was splashed with mud and obviously covered a lot more territory than a few miles along city streets.

Nick drove rapidly, in complete silence, for which Cassie was thankful. With thoughts of Alice alone and frightened uppermost in both minds, and mutual hostility latent beneath the surface all the time, polite conversation was impossible.

When they parked in a road lined with large, private homes, Cassie's spirits rose as she saw a light in one of the ground-floor rooms in Max's house.

Nick rang the bell, and kept his finger on it, but there was no response.

'There must be someone there,' said Cassie urgently. 'The light's on.'

'Automatic for security, like the outside lights,' said Nick briefly. He shivered in the icy wind as he bent to peer through the brass letterbox. 'Alice!' he called. 'It's Uncle Nick. Are you there, darling?' He turned to Cassie. 'You call. Perhaps a woman's voice will be more reassuring.'

Cassie bent at once, holding the flap open to shout through it. 'Alice, it's Cassie. Don't be frightened.' After calling a few times more, she straightened and turned to Nick. 'No use. Haven't you got a key?'

'Of course I haven't,' he snapped.

'It was just a thought.' Cassie hugged her arms across her chest. 'So what now?'

'I'm going to the police. Shall I take you home first?'

'Not on your life!' she flashed at him. 'I'm coming with you—' She halted suddenly. 'I've just thought of something.'

'What?'

'Julia.'

'What about her?'

'She might still have a key.'

Nick rubbed a hand over his jaw. 'She was the first one I thought of when I couldn't track Alice down. That's why I came round to your place.'

'I knew you didn't come to see me!'

'Look,' he said angrily, 'I may not be your favourite person, Cassandra Lovell, but believe me, I'm genuinely worried about Alice.'

'I do believe you,' she assured him. 'And I'm just as worried as you are. But if you're thinking that Julia's got her, you're wrong. Max doesn't allow her to see Alice, remember.'

'I'm hardly likely to forget!' he retorted, and turned up the collar of his raincoat. 'In the meantime we're freezing out here. Let's get in the car.'

'We'd better drive over to Julia's, just in case,' said Cassie reluctantly, as Nick started the car.

'In case she has a key, or in case she has Alice?'

'A key!' she said indignantly. 'It's best to make sure Alice isn't right here at home before dashing off to the police.'

Julia Lovell Seymour lived in the ground-floor flat of a small terraced house in Acton.

'We should have rung first,' said Cassie tersely as she pressed the buzzer.

'She would never have let me through the door,' said Nick grimly.

'Do you blame her?' said Cassie scornfully, then listened as her sister's voice answered warily. 'It's only me, Julia.'

'Cassie? I thought you had a heavy date tonight.'

'It fell through. Let me in, please.'

Cassie went into the house ahead of Nick, who stopped dead in his tracks as Julia came towards them like an avenging fury.

'What in the world are *you* doing here, Dominic Seymour?' Julia demanded in a fierce undertone. 'Be quiet,' she added, 'or you'll wake her.' She beckoned them into a small kitchen and closed the door behind them, turning on her sister angrily. 'Now then, Cassie, what are you playing at?'

'She's asleep?' said Nick eagerly.

Julia gave him a hostile look. She wore an unflattering navy dressing gown, and under the harsh striplight her violet eyes were deeply shadowed, her face tired and pale under gleaming hair the exact shade of the gilt streaks in Cassie's.

'Why did you tell him, Cassie?' she said accusingly.

'Tell me what?' demanded Nick.

'I didn't tell him anything, Julia,' said Cassie quickly. 'We've come about Alice.'

'Alice?' Julia's eyes widened in alarm. 'What's the matter? Is something wrong?'

'She's not here, then,' said Nick in despair, suddenly haggard as the colour drained from his face, leaving it sallow beneath the tan.

'Of course she isn't!' said Julia hotly. 'Your brother

won't let me near her—but never mind that, what's happened?'

Her pallor increased as she listened to Cassie's terse explanation.

'You mean Max is stuck in some jungle somewhere instead of taking care of his daughter?' She gave a short, mirthless laugh. 'And *I'm* the one who's deemed not fit to look after her!' Her face crumpled suddenly, and she clutched at Cassie. 'Surely there's been some mistake?'

'We came to see if you still had a key to the house,' said Nick with constraint.

Julia rounded on him, eyes flashing through sudden tears. 'To see if I'd stolen Alice, you mean!'

He shook his head vehemently. 'Not stolen, Julia. I hoped to God you did have her.'

'But I don't, I don't—' Julia snatched a tissue from a box and wiped her eyes. 'Although, unknown to Max, I *do* still have a key. After I locked myself out of the house in Chiswick once I had a spare made.'

'We thought there might be messages on Max's machine,' said Cassie, wanting badly to cuddle her sister, but knowing Julia wouldn't appreciate it in front of her tense brother-in-law. And Dominic Seymour was very obviously having difficulty in reconciling this pale, weary woman with the Julia he'd last seen as his brother's glamorous, beautiful wife in surroundings far removed from these.

Julia searched her handbag and produced a Yale key. 'I wish I could come with you to see if Alice is all right,' she said anxiously, as she handed it to Nick. 'But under the circumstances—' She looked up as a cry came from a distance.

'Let me,' said Cassie eagerly, and Julia hesitated, then nodded, resigned.

Cassie left Nick and Julia, eyeing each other like boxers shaping up for a fight, and went along the hall to a bedroom where a nightlight showed a little figure standing up in a cot. When the child caught sight of Cassie she smiled widely and held up her arms.

'Hello, Cassie! Where Mummy?'

Cassie scooped up the little body, caught up a blanket and wrapped her in it and cuddled her close. 'Hi, Emily. How's my gorgeous girl?'

The child chuckled, her face bright with a victorious smile as Cassie bore her off to the kitchen to meet Dominic Seymour.

'I see you were putty in her hands as usual,' said Julia dryly, and gazed at Nick with defiant eyes. 'I don't believe you've met my daughter, Nick. This is Emily.'

Nick stared at the child wildly, then at Julia and Cassie. 'No one told me.'

'Why should they?' said Cassie, nuzzling her niece's feathery curls.

'I don't understand,' said Nick blankly. 'If you were expecting his child why in hell did Max break up with you, Julia?'

'He thought she was yours,' she said without emotion.

'Mine?' Nick stared from Julia's beautiful, haggard face to the smooth, rosy cheeks of the little girl. 'Has he ever seen her?'

'Of course not,' said Cassie scornfully.

'Max must be mad. The nearest I ever got to Julia was to put an arm round her shoulders once. And we all know what happened after that,' said Nick grimly, then his eyes softened as the child eyed him curiously. 'But just look at her! She's the image of Max—a lot like Alice, in fact.' His eyes darkened. 'And Alice is missing.'

'Right, let's be on our way.' Cassie gave Emily a kiss and returned her to her mother. 'Thanks for the key, Julia.'

'Ring me as soon as you find out anything,' ordered Julia urgently, hugging her small daughter so tightly Emily protested a little.

'I will,' promised Cassie. 'Night-night, Emily. See you tomorrow.'

Emily flapped her hand, beaming. 'Ni-night, Cassie.' She turned large green eyes on Nick. 'Bye-bye.'

Nick waved back automatically, his eyes riveted on the child's face, then thanked Julia and said goodbye.

The moment they were back in the car he began demanding explanations. 'Why the hell didn't anyone *tell* me?' he said eventually. 'When my brother deigns to put in an appearance I'll tell him a few home truths, the stupid idiot.'

Cassie let out a screech, clutching at the door handle as they hurtled round a corner. 'Slow down, or you'll get the police after you. Anyway, when Max came home and caught you with Julia—'

'It wasn't like that!'

'Whatever you were doing, Max couldn't take it. After he threw you out he went berserk when Julia told him she was pregnant, and utterly refused to believe the child was his. He told Julia the marriage was over and she couldn't see Alice again. Which,' added Cassie with passion, 'was cruel. Julia had been Alice's stepmother for only a year, it's true, but she'd been working in the house for a long time before that as his secretary. They adored each other. The poor little thing was only six years old. It hurt Julia horribly.' She gave Nick a straight look. 'It didn't do Alice much good either. And now we haven't a clue where Alice is, and your brother is too busy with some prehistoric tribe to come home to his daughter, let alone care that he has another one he's never seen.'

CHAPTER TWO

WHEN they arrived in Chiswick, Max Seymour's house was as quiet and deserted as before.

'Let's hope he hasn't changed the locks,' said Nick grimly.

Cassie sighed with relief as Nick gave a grunt of triumph and opened the door, then switched on lights to reveal an undecorated Christmas tree standing in a bucket near the foot of the stairs, looking incongruous in the panelled hall.

'Alice!' yelled Nick, and took the stairs to the upper floor, two at a time. Cassie started after him, then changed her mind as she saw red lights glowing on the telephone on the hall table. With no compunction for listening to Max Seymour's private business, she pressed the button, her disappointment intense when she heard the voice of his agent, saying he needed to see Max the minute he got back from New Guinea.

You're not the only one, she thought grimly, then a familiar small voice made her heart beat faster.

'No one here,' said Nick, running down the stairs.

Cassie hushed him frantically as Alice's voice sounded on the machine. 'Hello, Daddy, this is Alice. I'm in Janet's house. Mrs Cartwright wanted to take me home with Laura, but I wanted to wait here for you. Janet was here, so I wasn't on my own. When you didn't come Janet said best to go home with her for the night and come back tomorrow, because she's got to cook Ken's supper. Come and fetch me when you get home,' ended Alice, on a quavering note which tore at Cassie's heartstrings.

'When he does I'll punch him in the nose,' said Nick savagely.

'Who's Janet?'

'She looks after the house for Max. She lives in during school holidays, but Ken, whoever he is, obviously had a prior claim tonight.'

'Where does she live?'

'Damned if I know. Let's find out.' Nick strode across the hall into a masculine, book-lined study dominated by a desk with a computer.

'So this is where he writes the books,' said Cassie, feeling a lot better now she knew Alice was safe.

Nick was rummaging through desk drawers at top speed, and seized on a leather address book. 'Bullseye. I was afraid Max might have kept everything on disk.' He flipped over pages swiftly, then frowned.

'What is it?' demanded Cassie impatiently. 'Isn't Janet there?'

'Yes, she is,' he said slowly. 'Her name's Jenkins.'

'Is there a telephone number for her?'

Nick nodded, and began punching out numbers on his phone as he handed Cassie the book. 'Read the other entry under "J".'

She shot him a curious look, then ran her eye over the other names, her teeth catching in her lower lip as her sister's name sprang out from the page. She held her breath as Nick began talking to someone on the phone, then let it out thankfully when his eyes blazed with relief.

'No, don't wake her up, Janet,' he was saying. 'I'm just glad Alice is safe with you. No, I'm afraid there's no news of her father yet. In the morning tell her I'll come round here to Chiswick about eleven, if that's convenient. Thank you very much indeed. Goodnight.'

Nick sat down very suddenly in the captain's chair behind his brother's desk. 'Thank God. Janet's bringing her back here in the morning.' He looked at Cassie levelly. 'So you've found Julia's address in there.'

Cassie nodded. 'The odd thing is, Nick, it's the Acton address, and she moved there only recently. He's obviously keeping tabs on her.'

Nick got up, frowning. 'On the baby, too?'

'I don't know.' Cassie gave him a wobbly smile. 'But don't let Emily hear you say "baby". She's a *big* girl.' Suddenly the events of the night all closed in on Cassie at once, and to her utter horror tears began rolling down her cheeks.

'Hey!' said Nick in alarm. 'Don't cry, Cassie. Please!' He seized her in his arms, but the tears only flowed faster, soaking his thin suit jacket. 'Look, if you don't stop I'll catch pneumonia. I'm not dressed for this weather—I'm freezing. If I get wet on top of it I'll be in trouble.'

Cassie pulled herself together and pushed him away, sniffing hard as she rummaged in her pocket for a tissue 'Sorry about that. Reaction. I kept imagining such terrible things—'

'Don't!' said Nick harshly. 'Alice is safe; that's all that counts.'

'Can I borrow your phone to ring Julia, please?' Cassie's reddened eyes flashed angrily. 'I won't use anything belonging to Max.'

Nick listened unashamedly as Cassie spoke reassuringly to her sister.

'Thanks,' she said briefly, handing the phone back.

'You could have talked longer than that, Cassie.'

'I couldn't. Julia was crying too much. With relief, like me.' Cassie sniffed inelegantly and rubbed at her eyes. 'At least she can get to sleep now. And, if Emily permits, maybe have a bit of a lie-in tomorrow as it's Saturday.'

'What happens in the week?'

'Julia works for a software manufacturer. The company provides a crèche where she can leave Emily.'

Nick scowled. 'She's got a job? No wonder she looks so exhausted.'

'How else would she manage? Babies are expensive.'

He looked uncomfortable. 'Forgive me for prying, but your parents live in the country. Wouldn't they prefer it if she returned home to live?'

'You bet they would! She did go home to have the baby, but when Emily was six months old Julia insisted on going back to work. Mother and Dad help as much as she allows, but Julia's very independent. She feels she's to blame for this mess—'

'It's my fault, not Julia's!'

'I blame Max,' said Cassie with venom. 'In fact, I could murder him with my bare hands at this precise moment.'

'That makes two of us,' he agreed. 'Let's get out of here. I don't know about you, but I'm starving.' He smiled suddenly, the first real smile he'd managed all night. 'Sorry I ruined your evening, Cassie. I'll buy you dinner to make amends.'

Cassie caught sight of herself in the mirror on Max's wall, and laughed. 'With red eyes and mascara smudges? No way. Thanks just the same.'

'You're not quite the vision who let me in earlier on,' agreed Nick, amused, as he locked up. 'But I think I prefer the way you look right now—more like the young Cassie I used to know.'

'You didn't know me at all, Dominic Seymour!' Which was all to the good, she thought with a shiver. If he had he might have noticed the crush she'd had on him once.

'Cold?' he said with sympathy, and turned the heater on full-blast.

Cassie settled low in her seat for the journey back to Shepherd's Bush, feeling hungry, emotionally drained and in no mood for conversation. A mood which Nick obviously shared. When they reached the house he manoeuvred the Subaru into a space better suited to a Mini, then killed the engine and turned to her.

'Cassie, I want to come in for a minute. I won't keep you long. I need some advice.'

Cassie had rather hoped to see him off right away. Now the crisis was over she felt tired and hungry and in need of her bed. And oddly flat. 'I suppose so,' she said, resigned.

Once inside the house she hung up her coat on a peg with Nick's raincoat, and because he was still shivering she turned the heating back on and took him into the kitchen, where it was warmest.

'Before dishing out this advice you're after,' she said, yawning, 'I'd better call Rupert and let him know Alice is safe.'

'Does he know Alice?'

'No. But he was very good about being pushed off without the meal I'd promised. And he did ask me to let him know what happened.' Cassie marched past Nick and shut the kitchen door behind her so she could talk to Rupert in private. But he wasn't home. Disappointed, she left a message, then went back to the kitchen to find

Nick munching on a hunk of bread he'd cut from the loaf on the table.

'Hope you don't mind,' he said indistinctly.

'Oh, for heaven's sake,' she said impatiently. 'If you're that hungry I'll give you a proper meal. But don't kid yourself I feel any friendlier towards you, Nick. It's only because I'm famished myself.'

Nick's eyes glittered coldly, but instead of refusing, as Cassie expected, he forced a smile. 'If you're sure it's no trouble.'

'I wouldn't offer if it was,' she assured him. 'It won't take long.'

'Thanks, Cassie. Mind if I have some more bread?'

'Help yourself,' she said, resigned, and lit the gas under the soup and the vegetables. She handed him a bottle of wine and a corkscrew. 'Open that, please,' she ordered, then went out to fetch the silverware and plates from the other room. The splendour of the red cloth and the candles had been for Rupert. Nick Seymour could make do with the kitchen.

He smiled sardonically as she set the table. 'Ah! The honour of candles and tablecloth is not to be mine.'

'No,' she said shortly.

'This is cosier,' he assured her. 'After all, we're sort of family, you and I, Cassie.'

Her eyes flashed. 'You mean you're in love with your brother's wife, who just happens to be my sister.'

For a moment Cassie was afraid she'd gone too far, but Nick held on to his temper with obvious, rather frightening effort.

'You're wrong!' he said harshly at last. 'I was a bit of a fool about Julia when I was younger, I admit, but she only had eyes for Max—always. Once they were married I steered clear of the house unless invited. I called unexpectedly that particular day because I was off to work in Nigeria for a while. I found Julia feeling off-colour and miserable because Max was about to leave on one of his endless trips into some wilderness, so I gave her a hug. Max walked in on a bit of brotherly comfort on my part and the rest is history.' He looked Cassie in the eye. 'I had a callow, immature crush on Julia once, it's true. But it died a natural death. On the day in question I was just providing a convenient shoulder to cry on.'

'It's a pity you never managed to convince your brother of the fact,' she pointed out, stirring the soup.

'I tried, believe me,' said Nick wearily. 'No one was more appalled by what happened than I was.'

'I seriously doubt that!' Cassie slid the salmon into the microwave and fetched soup bowls from the cupboard. 'The effect on Julia was shattering.'

'I know. She refused to have anything to do with me afterwards. I haven't seen her since, until tonight.' He looked up, the striking blue eyes full of remorse. 'She looks so much older, Cassie.'

'So would you if you were a single parent juggling a lively toddler with a demanding job,' she retorted. 'Besides, Julia doesn't usually look like that. You caught her at the end of a long working week, trying to get her baby to sleep. She was entitled to look tired.'

Nick nodded morosely, then brightened visibly as Cassie brought bowls of hot, fragrant soup to the table. 'This smells wonderful. I'm impressed.'

'I aim to please,' she said briskly, sitting down. 'Have some more bread.'

Cassie was almost as hungry as Nick, and neither of them said much until the soup bowls were empty. But when she put a plate of salmon and vegetables in front of him Nick gave her a wry look.

'This was intended for Ashcroft, of course. I'm hellish sorry I ruined your evening, Cassie.'

She shrugged philosophically. 'There'll be other times. I see Rupert every day, anyway.'

'So this is a regular occurrence?' Nick began on his meal with relish. 'If so, he's a lucky guy.'

Cassie poured wine into their glasses, her resentment flaring up again. 'Actually this was our first real date. I haven't known Rupert long. He's taken me out for a drink after work sometimes, but when he asked me out to dinner I suggested he came round here instead. So tonight was rather special.'

'And I wrecked it.' Nick drank some wine, his eyes sombre. 'Something I'm bloody good at where the Lovells are concerned.'

'Oh, get on with your supper,' she said irritably. 'After all,' she added, trying to be fair, 'when it comes to wrecking lives it was Max who did the demolition job on Julia's, not you.'

'He's not doing much better with Alice, either, if today is anything to go by,' said Nick grimly. 'Let's talk about something else. You, preferably. I know you went to college. What did you read?'

'I did a BA in secretarial administration.' Cassie added more vegetables to Nick's plate.

'And after that?' he prompted. 'Go on. I'm interested.'

'I did temping for a while. I liked the variety, and it gave me experience, and a chance to find a job I really liked. These days I provide administrative support to a team of eight at an investment bank in the City. The group analyses the credit quality of various companies and so on.'

'And young Rupert is one of the team,' stated Nick.

'Yes.' Cassie frowned at him. 'And he's only a couple of years younger than you, Nick Seymour.'

'And what exactly is this "support" you give Rupert?'

'Exactly what the rest of the team gets,' she said evenly. 'All of them travel a lot, and I spend hours on the phone organising their itineraries and co-ordinating meetings.'

Nick grinned. 'So it's not just a spot of dictation and typing, then.'

'No. I have all the usual keyboard skills, of course,' said Cassie loftily, 'but I use them to draft letters and presentations, mainly. I love my involvement in the job. I was able to smooth Rupert's path quite a lot when he joined the team.'

'As I said, lucky guy. Are you in love with him?' added Nick casually.

Instead of snubbing him, Cassie thought it over. 'I'm certainly attracted to him,' she said at last.

'When I arrived the scene looked set for a very intimate evening, Cassie. Was he hoping to take you to bed at the end of it?'

'It's none of your business!' she said angrily.

'I apologise, Cassie,' Nick said promptly, and gave her a hopeful smile. 'Would there be pudding by any chance?'

'You've got a nerve,' she said, shaking her head as she got up to take his plate. 'As it happens I do have a pudding for once—*tartelet aux cerises*, to be precise.'

'Cherry tart—wonderful!' he said with relish. 'I don't seem to have eaten much these past few days.'

'Why not?'

'There were hold-ups on a hotel construction in

Riyadh. I've been on site there for the last two months, troubleshooting and generally getting everything back on schedule. I've been working all hours so I could get back to the UK for Christmas.' Nick's eyes gleamed as Cassie served him the warmed tart with a spoonful of whipped cream. 'That looks good. My Somali cook out there had certain specialities he served at every meal. I'd be happy never to see a jacket potato again.'

'They're my staple diet,' said Cassie. She topped up his wine glass and leaned back in her chair. 'Four minutes or so in a microwave, a spoonful of cottage cheese, and dinner's ready.'

'So you don't cook like this every night?'

She chuckled. 'I don't cook like this any night.'

His eyebrows rose. 'You mean you had this sent in?'

'No. I just bought it all on the way home and read the instructions on the packets. I had my hair done instead. Much more important than slaving over a hot stove.'

Nick threw back his head and laughed, and suddenly he was so much more like the young man Cassie had once fancied so much she felt a pang of nostalgia for times past, before Max's jealousy had disrupted so many lives.

'Were you going to admit all that to young Ashcroft?' he demanded.

'Only if he asked,' said Cassie honestly. 'I was hoping he'd be too fascinated by my company and my appearance to care where the meal came from.'

'As he was!' said Nick emphatically. 'I walked in on how fascinated he was.' He sobered suddenly. 'Was the dress new, bought specially for the occasion?'

Cassie nodded, the look in his dark-rimmed blue eyes putting her on guard. 'Yes. Why?'

'I feel more of a heel than ever. You obviously spent

a lot of money on a dress and your hair, not to mention the meal—'

'If you bang on about ruining my evening again, I'll throw my plate at you,' she said irritably. 'Finding Alice was a lot more important than any dress, and if it makes you any happier you can jolly well pay for the meal, since you've eaten most of it, Dominic Seymour.'

'All right, all right,' he said hastily. 'Pax, Cassie. If I'm paying, can I have some more wine? I've been living without such niceties these past few weeks.'

'You've got to drive home,' she reminded him.

'How *have* I organised my life without you up to now?' he said with sarcasm, and commandeered the bottle to pour himself a second glass of wine. 'If it won't inconvenience you too much, Cassandra Lovell, I'll leave the car here and take a cab tonight. Alcohol doesn't play a big part in my life, but after the shock of finding Alice missing is it a sin to fancy a glass of wine or two? Especially after two months of abstinence?'

'No, of course not. Sorry.' She shook her head when he made to refill her glass. 'Not for me, thanks. I'll make some coffee later. Bring the bottle and your glass and we'll go and sit in the other room. You look tired.'

Nick got up, yawning. 'Life's been pretty hectic lately.' He followed her into the other room and sank down on the sofa with a sigh after she curled up in a chair. He eyed her gloomily. 'What the hell am I going to do, Cassie?'

'About Alice?'

'Yes. And Max, too. Frankly, I'm worried. There's been some unrest near the particular region he was heading for. I hope he hasn't got tangled up in any of it.'

'So do I!' Cassie shivered. 'Though only because of Alice,' she added with candour.

Nick was silent for a long interval, smiling his thanks when Cassie refilled his glass. 'What the blazes *am* I going to do? How the devil do I provide a proper Christmas for Alice? I hope Janet's willing to hang on in Chiswick. If she is I'd better take over one of Max's spare rooms until he turns up. Whether he likes it or not,' he added grimly. 'We've seen as little as possible of each other since the break-up with Julia, but he lets me see Alice now and then.'

'As well he might,' said Cassie indignantly. 'With no grandparents any more, the poor little thing's not exactly awash with relatives!'

Nick frowned. 'If Julia's so fond of Alice, how has Max managed to keep her away from her?'

'He was in such a rage that memorable day he actually threatened her with an injunction. But there are ways round that. I take letters and presents from Julia when I take Alice out from school. So does my mother.' Cassie sighed angrily. 'Your brother's inhuman.'

'Step-brother, actually,' Nick reminded her.

'Oh, yes. I'd forgotten that. You certainly don't resemble each other.'

'Max looks like his mother. She ran off with another man when he was a baby, so Dad hired a very highly qualified nanny by the name of Eileen Ryan, and fell in love with her. He married her as soon as the divorce came through, and a year or so later I was born.'

'I've seen her photograph,' said Cassie quietly. 'You're the image of her.'

'I know. I miss her. I miss them both. So does Max. Which,' said Nick, with sudden violence, 'is why I can never understand why he keeps Julia away from Alice. He loved my mother, and she loved him. Just as Julia loves Alice.'

'Perhaps it's pride.'

'Maybe he expects every woman to behave like his biological mother.'

Cassie pulled out the shoelace from her hair, which she'd grabbed from one of her sneakers in her hurry to look for Alice. The gleaming ringlets cascaded to the shoulders of her dark blue sweater, and she tugged on one of them absently with her teeth as a plan began to formulate in her mind. She looked up to see Nick's eyes on her.

'What?' she demanded.

'I was admiring the view.' A smile tugged at the corners of his wide, well-cut mouth. 'Poor Rupert.'

'What do you mean?'

'I'm just beginning to realise what he's missed out on tonight. A great meal—wherever it came from—and a beautiful companion to enjoy it with.' He sighed theatrically. 'I should feel guilty, but I don't—even if I am just an interloper who got lucky.'

'This is as lucky as you get,' she warned him sharply, put out by something in his manner.

The spectacular eyes gleamed. 'Don't worry, Cassie. I wasn't about to leap on your body.'

'I'm glad to hear it,' she retorted, bristling. 'I prefer men who come without your history, Dominic Seymour.'

'Why does my name sound like an epithet when you say it in full?' he asked curiously.

'It's better than some epithets I could use!'

'So you still dislike me?'

She shrugged. 'I'm not crazy about you, I admit. Though Julia told me you weren't really to blame for what happened. I know you were in love with her once, of course, but that was nothing new. Most men she met fell in love with her. I just wish she'd married any one of them instead of Max Seymour.'

'Does she still feel the same way about him?' asked Nick soberly.

'We don't discuss Max, but I'm pretty sure she does. Though how she can still love him utterly mystifies me. If a man treated me like that I'd either murder him or forget he ever existed.'

'No grand passion for you, then, Cassie?'

'No way. I'm not the type.' She shrugged. 'I quite fancy Rupert, but I don't see him as something permanent in my life.'

Nick got to his feet, yawning. 'I'll withdraw to your bathroom, then I'd better call a cab.'

'I'll make some coffee first,' she said, jumping up.

'What a saint you are, Cassandra,' he mocked, and breathed in deeply to steady himself as he followed her from the room.

Cassie went out to fill Meg's expensive Italian machine with the Blue Mountain coffee she'd bought to impress Rupert. While it was brewing she washed up quickly, obeying the golden rule of the house. No dirty dishes left until next day. At last she filled tall mugs with fragrant dark coffee, and put them on a tray with cream and sugar.

Cassie nudged the sitting-room door open with her knee, then gave a sigh of pure frustration, mentally kicking herself for taking so long. Nick Seymour was stretched out on the sofa, fast asleep.

Cassie muttered something rude under her breath, put the tray down on the table and did her best to rouse Nick from a sleep so deep it looked like a coma. And it might just as well have been for all the good it did when she tried to wake him. In the end she gave up, bone-weary herself by this time. She took the tray back into the kitchen, gulped down some of her coffee and went upstairs to borrow a blanket and a double quilt from Hannah, who was skiing with Meg in Gstaad. Cassie eased Nick's shoes from his long, chilly feet, put a cushion under his head and tucked the blanket and quilt round his sprawled, relaxed body, careless of whether she disturbed him. But Nick slumbered on, vanquished by a combination of jet-lag and stress topped off by a good dinner and three glasses of unaccustomed wine.

'Sweet dreams,' said Cassie, resigned, and turned out the light.

CHAPTER THREE

CASSIE surfaced next morning to find a scantily clad Polly shaking her awake.

'You're nuts, Cassie Lovell,' her friend stated, eyes dancing, and perched on the bed. 'What's the point of wining and dining this Rupert person if you make him sleep on the sofa?'

'Oh, heavens,' gasped Cassie, the events of last night flooding back in full flow. 'He's still there?'

'Sleeping like a babe. Though more sexy pirate than baby.' Polly rolled her eyes. 'I can see why you were so steamed up about getting him to yourself, ducky. Why on earth did you banish him to the sofa?'

'I didn't,' said Cassie tersely, scrambling out of bed. 'He fell asleep while I was making coffee.'

'Oh, bad luck,' said her friend with sympathy. 'Was Rupert tired after a long day at the bank or something?'

'No.' Cassie shrugged on her dressing gown. 'The man downstairs isn't Rupert.' She chuckled wickedly as Polly's mouth fell open. 'His name is Dominic Seymour—*ducky*. He's my sister's brother-in-law, but never mind that, I'll explain later. And put some clothes on, Polly. A good thing Nick didn't wake up if you barged in on him like that. He's been working abroad without a drink or feminine company for a couple of months.'

'How scrummy—I wish I'd known!' said the irrepressible Polly, dodging the pillow Cassie hurled at her.

After a short interval in the bathroom, Cassie rushed

back to her room to drag a brush through the tousled ringlets, then, ignoring Polly's entreaties to tell all, she raced downstairs as she was, shivering in her striped pyjamas and old blue dressing gown. She turned the heating up and went into the sitting-room to find Nick still out for the count, his mouth open slightly, but not snoring. It was the only point in his favour. The growth of black stubble along his jaw had grown thicker overnight—Polly wasn't far wrong with her pirate description. 'Sleeping like a babe' was hardly applicable. There was nothing helpless about Nick Seymour, awake or asleep.

Cassie shook him ungently and tried to pull the covers off, but Nick muttered ominously and held on like grim death, refusing to wake. With a sigh of exasperation Cassie went over to the windows and drew back the curtains on a sunny, frosty morning, the bright light doing more to penetrate Nick's consciousness than all her shaking. He sat up suddenly, blinking like an owl as he saw Cassie standing over him, arms folded and a militant expression on her face.

'The usual line is "where am I?",' she informed him tartly.

Nick shot to his feet, shivering, and rubbed his jaw in distaste. 'I know where I am, Cassie, but why the hell am I still here?'

'It wasn't my choice, believe me,' she assured him. 'But when you sleep, you certainly sleep, Dominic Seymour. I couldn't rouse you last night so I left you there. I hoped you'd wake up in the night and tactfully take yourself off. Instead you gave one of my fellow tenants a nasty shock this morning.'

He grimaced. 'Sorry. I'll apologise later. At the moment I need a bathroom. I don't suppose you'd have a spare toothbrush?'

'Polly might. I'll find out.'

Polly, now fully dressed in skin-tight leather trousers and a curve-hugging ribbed sweater, was happy to oblige. 'Always keep one for emergencies, pet,' she said cheerfully, rummaging in a drawer. 'Would Bluebeard like to borrow a razor, too, while I make breakfast?'

Nick accepted both offerings from Cassie with gratitude, and came downstairs later, hair relatively tidy and his jaw clean-shaven. Despite his rumpled clothes, he looked a lot better, and to the impressionable Polly obviously very fanciable indeed.

'Hi, I'm Polly Cooper,' she informed him jauntily. 'Want some coffee?'

'Nick Seymour,' he returned, with a dazzling smile. 'I'm told I gave you a shock earlier. My apologies.'

Polly assured him she'd suffered no ill effects.

Cassie took her eyes off the toast under the grill. 'Want some breakfast, Nick?'

'If you don't think I've trespassed too much on your hospitality already,' he said wryly, sitting at the table.

'A few minutes more won't matter, I suppose,' said Cassie. She put the toast rack on the table and handed him a sales-slip from the well-known source of the previous night's dinner. 'I'm sure you'll enjoy breakfast more if you settle up for this.'

'Cassie!' remonstrated Polly in horror. 'You're not making him *pay* for his dinner?'

'Why not? It was meant for Rupert,' said Cassie, filling three coffee mugs. She pushed the butter towards Nick.

'I ruined her evening, so she's entitled to make me

pay. Though I think it's for more than just dinner,' added Nick, looking Cassie in the eye.

'I was joking,' she muttered, and snatched the sales-slip back.

Nick looked unconvinced. 'Right. I'll just finish this and be on my way. I need a bath and a change of clothes before I pick up Alice.'

'Will you come back for me?' asked Cassie.

'Is that what you want?'

Polly looked on in fascination as the two pairs of eyes locked, one pair dark-rimmed blue, still shadowed with fatigue, thc other pair oval, the velvety brown irises surprisingly dark below the fair hair.

Cassie nodded. 'I've got something to suggest. So if you get back here in an hour it should give us time to talk before fetching Alice.'

Nick glanced at his watch, then finished his coffee quickly. 'I'll get off, then. I'll be back as soon as I can.'

'Wow!' said Polly after Nick had gone. 'Why have you never mentioned *him* before?'

Polly was a recent addition to the household. Knowing she wouldn't let it rest, Cassie gave her the bare bones of her acquaintance with Dominic Seymour, leaving out the fact that he was in some way to blame for the break-up of Julia's marriage. And when Cassie added the worry of the night before over Alice, Polly was full of sympathy.

'Poor little thing. You'd think her father could have got home in time for Christmas.'

'He may do yet—still four days to go.'

'And what happens in the meantime?' demanded Polly. 'Will this housekeeper person look after her? Or does Nick have a girlfriend likely to lend a hand?'

'No idea, on both counts. I hope we can sort something out later. Whatever happens,' added Cassie firmly, 'I'm going to see Alice this morning, let her know there are people who care about her.'

When Nick returned later, dressed in a cream twill shirt and heavy navy sweater with thick-ribbed cords and a fleece-lined suede jacket, he looked considerably better.

'Polly's gone shopping,' said Cassie, letting him in. 'Jane, another friend you haven't met yet, stayed overnight with the boyfriend, so we've got the place to ourselves for a bit. We need to talk.'

'I know.' He shrugged out of his jacket and hung it on a peg in the hall with a familiarity Cassie noted with disapproval. She didn't want Nick Seymour to feel he was part of the scene in the house. This was *her* territory.

'I'll get the coffee. You can resume your former place on the sofa,' she said firmly. 'Won't be a moment.'

When she returned with a tray Nick was eyeing the arrangement Cassie had finally achieved with Rupert's flowers.

'From your merchant banker,' he commented.

'Lovely, aren't they?' She put the tray down on the table beside them and handed Nick a mug. 'Sugar? Milk?'

'No, thanks.'

Cassie waved him to the sofa and curled up in her usual chair. During Nick's absence she'd showered and dressed in a white shirt and russet wool sweater with a short tweed skirt. She wore thick, patterned wool tights and gleaming chestnut leather boots, and a broad brown velvet ribbon did its best to restrain her hair.

Nick eyed the result with unconcealed approval. 'Are you meeting Rupert today?' he asked.

'No.' Though Cassie had hoped to.

Nick got up restlessly, losing interest in Rupert. 'Cassie, I'm hellish worried. There's no news of Max, and Christmas is only four days away. I'll move into the house in Chiswick, of course, but it's going to be grim for Alice with just the two of us, poor kid.'

Cassie frowned. 'Isn't there a woman in your life these days?'

'Several I could ask out for the evening.' Nick's mouth twisted. 'But no one likely to help entertain a little girl.'

She nodded, unsurprised. Nick had never been short of female company, but in the past he'd been attracted more to social butterflies than earth mothers. 'In that case I've a plan to put forward. I made a couple of phone calls this morning as a contingency plan, in case there was no news of Max.'

Nick sat down again, his eyes intent. 'I'm grateful for any suggestion, Cassie, believe me.'

'First I rang Julia, then I rang my parents and explained the situation.'

'Their opinion of Max must be at a new low, then,' said Nick bitterly.

'Their concern was all for Alice.' Cassie brushed back a stray, escaping curl. 'My father is driving up from Gloucestershire to collect Julia and Emily today. Julia's staying at home in Chastlecombe until the New Year. I'm joining them on Christmas Eve.' She looked at Nick searchingly. 'Alice could go back with them, spend Christmas at home with all of us. If you agree.'

His eyes blazed with such gratitude Cassie was dazzled. 'It's not up to me to agree or not. But I think it's a fantastic idea.' He paused, sobering quickly. 'I'd have done my best for her, but she'd be so much better off with your mother and that cute little cherub of Julia's.

And if Max objects, what the hell?' He breathed in a deep sigh of relief. 'Cassie, you don't know what a load you've taken off my mind.'

'And you'll be free to keep to your own plans, of course,' she said, rather pointedly.

Nick's jaw tightened. 'My "plans", as you put it, involve a couple of days on my own in a hotel near Worcester, booked before I went to Saudi.'

Cassie stared at him in surprise. 'In that case Alice will definitely be better off with the rest of us in Chastlecombe.' She jumped to her feet. 'I'll ring home now and tell them you approve—'

'Would you mind if I spoke to your mother personally, to thank her?' he put in. 'Or do your parents regard me as the villain of the piece?'

'No. That's Max's role,' she assured him, then smiled suddenly. 'Don't tell her I told you, but Mother always had a soft spot for you, anyway.'

'That's music to my ears. I'm glad someone does,' he said morosely. 'You weren't exactly friendly last night—nor Julia.'

'Did you expect us to be?'

'I make it a rule, Cassie, to expect as little as possible. It saves disappointment,' he said bitingly, then looked at her very directly. 'It's a long time since I was in love with Julia, no matter what you think, but she's still someone I regard as very special. It was painful to see her in those circumstances last night. It hit me for six.'

'I could tell!' She picked up her large leather satchel bag. 'Right. Here's my address book. The number's on the first page, with Julia's.'

Cassie went into the kitchen with the tray, leaving Nick to talk to her mother—a conversation which obviously went well judging by his reluctance to hand over the receiver for her to confirm arrangements with her delighted parent.

'Mother's so relieved,' she told Nick as they got in the car. 'She's been worrying like mad over Alice's Christmas anyway. She went up like a rocket when she heard what happened last night.' She paused. 'Are we taking things for granted, Nick? We've been busy making arrangements on Alice's behalf, but we haven't consulted her in any way.'

'If she doesn't like the idea, I'll cancel my hotel booking and stay in Chiswick with her,' said Nick promptly. 'Whatever Alice decides, I'm grateful for your help, Cassie.'

'I've done nothing much—'

'On the contrary. You've organised everything, me included. This team you support is damn lucky.'

When they reached the house in Chiswick, Nick rang the doorbell. 'I'd like to hang on to the key,' he muttered. 'I don't want another scare like last night.'

The door was opened by a young woman dressed in jeans and jersey.

'Hello, Janet,' said Nick, smiling, and her pleasant face lit up with relief.

'Good morning, Mr Seymour. Sorry I worried you by making off with Alice last night, but my fiancé was coming home on leave from the Army, and I wanted to be there when he arrived.'

'Don't apologise, Janet. I'm just grateful you took care of Alice,' he assured her.

'She's ever so worried about her dad,' she whispered.

'I am too,' he admitted, and introduced Cassie.

'It's so nice to meet you at last,' said Janet, ushering them inside. 'I've heard such a lot about you from Alice.'

Suddenly there was the sound of flying feet and a small figure came hurtling down the stairs to throw herself at Nick, who leapt up to meet her halfway and picked her up, giving her a smacking kiss on both cheeks.

'Uncle Nick,' cried Alice Seymour, burying her face in his neck. 'Daddy hasn't come home.'

'I know, poppet. But he will, don't you worry. In the meantime, look who I've brought to see you.'

'Cassie!' cried the child with delight, and raced down into the arms held out to receive her.

When the hugs and kisses were over, Alice tugged Nick and Cassie by the hand to pull them towards the Christmas tree, which was half trimmed, with open boxes of baubles and tinsel scattered round it.

'We started on it this morning. I thought it would be nice to have it ready,' said Janet quietly.

'Brilliant idea,' agreed Cassie. 'Shall we finish it off together, darling?'

Alice agreed with enthusiasm, a lot less forlorn as she helped Cassie and Nick rummage in the boxes.

'I'll make some coffee then,' said Janet, and Nick jumped up.

'I'll help,' he said promptly. 'I need a word with you, Janet.'

Alice Seymour was a thin little girl, rather tall for her age, with a mop of short tawny curls, freckles, and eyes the colour of moss, just like her father, with no resemblance at all to the photograph of the pretty blonde young mother who'd died when she was born.

She chattered happily to Cassie as they worked, full of questions about Julia and Emily.

'I've got a present for Emily,' she confided. 'Janet helped me choose it. Will you give it to her, Cassie?'

'I may be able to do better than that, darling,' said Cassie, her eyes questioning as Nick came back with a coffee tray.

'I've told Janet the plan and she thinks it's a brilliant idea,' he announced.

'What plan, Uncle Nick?' said Alice excitedly. 'Is it something nice?'

'Very nice—' he began, then broke off as the phone rang.

Janet answered it, spoke briefly, then called Nick over, shaking her head in response to Alice's eager demand to know if it was Daddy. 'No, pet. It's Mrs Cartwright. Have you found the fairy yet? It must be in one of these boxes.'

'Mrs Cartwright sent her love,' said Nick, hunkering down beside Alice. 'I told her you were fine and she needn't worry. She says you can go round and spend time with Laura whenever you want.'

'Not today,' said Alice promptly, clutching Cassie's hand.

'No,' he agreed. 'Not today. After Christmas some time. Talking of which, Cassie's made a fantastic suggestion.' He drew her to the stairs, sat down on the bottom step and took her on his knee to warn her that Daddy might be held up in New Guinea and not be able to get back in time for Christmas. Alice smothered a sob, and leaned against him so miserably Cassie badly wanted to snatch her from Nick to comfort her. Her eyes met his over the curly head, and she turned away quickly, busying herself with the search for the missing fairy.

Nick quickly outlined the plan for Alice to spend Christmas in the Lovell household with Cassie and her parents. 'And Julia and Emily,' he added.

Alice sat bolt upright, staring at him in disbelief, then jumped up and ran to Cassie. 'Is it true?' she demanded passionately. 'Can I really have Christmas with Julia?'

At that moment, if Max Seymour had walked through the door Cassie would have caused him grievous bodily harm and revelled in it.

'You bet,' she said huskily. 'If your father can't get home for Christmas, I'm sure he'll be happy to know you're having a lovely time with my parents and me. And Julia and Emily, too,' she added.

At which point Janet went off to have a private cry in the kitchen, while a supercharged Alice, in transports of delight, hindered Cassie's efforts to finish decorating the Christmas tree, giggling wildly at Nick's mutterings as he tried to get the fairy lights to work. Afterwards they sent out for pizza, and enjoyed a lively, noisy lunch in the kitchen with Janet.

'I hope this New Guinea tribe of his eats Max for Christmas dinner,' said Cassie viciously, after Janet had taken Alice off to pack.

Nick grinned. 'I doubt they celebrate Christmas.' He sobered. 'It's all a bit sad, really. Max and I used to be quite close for stepbrothers. But since the break-up that's finished. I haven't been in the country much at the same time as Max since, but when I'm in the UK I take Alice out for the day as often as possible.'

'I know. She's told me all about her outings with Uncle Nick.' Cassie looked thoughtful. 'Are there any women in Max's life?'

Nick shrugged. 'Not as far as I know. Alice never mentions anyone. But he probably keeps that side of his life from her. Lord knows he has ample opportunity. Alice doesn't see much of him.'

'Some people,' said Cassie malevolently, 'shouldn't

be parents. Come on—let's hurry Janet up. Dad's due at my place with Julia in a few minutes, if everything's going to plan.'

After a grateful, emotional parting with Janet, the three of them set off for Shepherd's Bush in a general mood of euphoria which intensified when they found a familiar, battered Range Rover had arrived before them. It was a good ten years older than Rupert's, in need of a wash, and crammed with a highchair and baby seat, and a mound of luggage behind the wire mesh screen fitted to pen in the family dogs.

'They're here,' said Cassie. Alice, white with excitement, her freckles standing out in relief, followed close behind as Cassie unlocked the door to reveal her father and Emily in the hall on all fours, playing trains.

'Hi, Dad—be careful, you'll do yourself an injury!'

Her father jumped up, smiling sheepishly, and gave her a hug. 'Hello, sweetheart. Your friend Polly let us in.' He peered behind her at Alice, his smile broadening. 'And who's this grown-up young lady, may I ask? Not Alice, surely!'

Alice greeted him shyly, delighted when he gave her a smacking kiss, then she dropped on her knees in front of the toddler. 'Hello, Emily.'

'Lally!' said Emily, beaming.

Alice hugged her in delight. 'She remembers me, Cassie! And her hair's grown. It's like mine.'

'And the freckles,' said Cassie, aware that Nick was watching the little scene with narrowed eyes.

'I believe someone in the kitchen wants to see you, poppet,' Bill Lovell told Alice. 'You can play with Emily later.'

Alice gave her little sister another kiss, then jumped up and ran into the kitchen.

'Julia probably wants a private reunion,' said Cassie.

Nick nodded soberly, and gave her father a very direct look. 'This is very good of you, sir. Please thank Mrs Lovell again. I'm more grateful than I can say.'

'We're only too pleased to have Alice, but I hope it won't cause trouble between you and your brother,' said Mr Lovell bluntly.

'I'll take full responsibility,' Nick assured him.

Cassie opened the kitchen door, found her sister and Alice in close embrace, and withdrew again hastily. 'I'll leave them in peace for a bit.'

'Julia's in a bit of a state,' said Bill Lovell in an undertone. 'She won't admit it, but she's deeply worried because Max is missing. And at the same time she's afraid that if and when he does turn up he'll prevent Alice from spending Christmas with us. She was very uptight on the way over.'

Nick's face set in aggressive lines. 'If Max does turn up,' he said with emphasis, 'I'll make damn sure he doesn't spoil things—for Julia or Alice.'

It was an hour later before Bill Lovell finally stowed his precious cargo safely in the Range Rover. When Emily was strapped into her car seat in the back, with a radiant Alice buckled in beside her, Julia hugged Cassie, then gave Nick a dazzling smile as he handed her up into her seat.

'My thanks to both of you,' she said huskily, and turned to look at the two children in the back. 'OK, girls? Right, then, Dad—home, please!'

'See you on Christmas Eve,' called Cassie as the car drew away, and stood with Nick, waving until the shabby Range Rover turned the corner out of sight.

Nick, shivering as usual, went back indoors with her.

'I'm missing a few pieces of the jigsaw,' he said casually. 'I thought Julia wasn't supposed to see Alice.'

'I accidentally bump into Julia and Emily when I take Alice out from school for the day,' said Cassie defiantly. 'You can tell Max, if you like. Any time he wants to pick a fight with me over it I'm ready and willing, believe me.'

'I do, I do!' Nick threw up his hands in mock terror. 'Of course I won't tell Max. What do you take me for?' He paused. 'Alice never breathed a word to me.'

'It's our secret.' Cassie scowled. 'It's so awful, making a little girl keep secrets from her father.'

'Better than keeping Alice and Julia apart,' he assured her. He looked at his watch. 'Look, Cassie, I need a favour. There's still time to hit the shops. Come with me, and give advice. I haven't done any Christmas shopping, and I need something special for Alice and Emily, for starters.'

Cassie was secretly feeling rather flat after waving her family off. She'd wanted to go with them instead of waiting another three days. Jane and Polly had gone out with their current men, as they did most Saturdays. And Meg and Hannah were away on holiday. The rest of the afternoon stretched before her, with nothing to do. Nick Seymour wasn't her most favourite person in the world, but he had a car and time to spare, and she still had some shopping of her own to sort out.

'All right, on condition I shop for myself at the same time,' she said at last. 'Just give me a minute to tidy myself up and I'll come. But you'll have a terrible job to park anywhere.'

'Want to bet?'

CHAPTER FOUR

NICK'S strategy for Christmas shopping was to get it all done under one roof. And he won his bet. He found a parking space within reach of Harrods by the simple expedient of being on the spot when someone moved out of it.

'I had a girlfriend who lived round here,' he said, grinning. 'I know this neck of the woods quite well.'

'Along with several other London districts, for the same reason, I suppose!'

It had taken them longer than usual to drive from Shepherd's Bush to Knightsbridge, which resulted in a concentrated, high-speed shopping spree in the time left, due to Nick's determination to do it all at once.

'I'll be tied up on Monday, and the next day's Christmas Eve,' he pointed out, flourishing a credit card.

By the time they returned to the car, laden with bags and packages, Cassie was hot, untidy, but full of a strange exhilaration. And surprise, because the afternoon had been fun. Nick Seymour, thought of with hostility for the past couple of years—when thought of at all—had been great company. Most men got bored with shopping, according to friends with more experience in this field than Cassie. But, fresh from two months in the company of his own sex in the far reaches of Saudi Arabia, Nick had quite plainly enjoyed the whole thing.

'Have I worn you out?' he asked, as he stowed their purchases away in the car.

'I enjoyed it,' she said candidly. 'I just hope you aren't bankrupt after all that.'

'I don't have that many to buy for.'

'Just as well—some of that stuff was hugely expensive!'

When they got back to the house Nick brought all the packages in so they could disentangle Cassie's purchases from his.

'I didn't really intend to do so much shopping myself,' she said ruefully, as they laid their haul out on the sitting-room floor. 'Your enthusiasm was infectious.'

'A good thing you reminded me to buy wrapping paper and so on.' He frowned as he eyed the large Paddington Bear he'd bought for Emily. 'How on earth do I make a neat parcel of this chap?'

Cassie sighed, resigned. 'Look, are you in a hurry?'

'No. Why?'

'If you let me drink some tea first, I'll give you a hand to wrap this lot up. I'm getting a lift down to Chastlecombe, so I'll even deliver them for you. So if you just write tags and labels you've got Christmas sorted.'

'Not in quite the way I'd like best,' he said dryly, 'but from the gift point of view I'm in far better shape than I expected to be at this stage. All thanks to you, Cassie.'

'It was fun.' She took off her coat. 'Want some tea?'

'I certainly do. Thanks.' He took her coat and hung it up with his jacket in the hall, then followed her into the kitchen. 'Where are your room-mates?'

'Two of them are on holiday, and Polly was dragging her current swain to a film this afternoon, followed by dinner and a club somewhere. I'm not sure of Jane's programme, except that she won't be back tonight.' Cassie made tea, poured some into mugs and handed one to Nick, surprising a speculative look on his face. 'What?' she demanded.

'How about you, Cassie? Surely you weren't planning to spend Saturday night alone?'

He was right. Cassie had fondly expected a date with Rupert, as a natural progression from the evening before. But her carefully laid plans for Rupert had gone pear-shaped the moment Dominic Seymour came storming into her life again. And she had a feeling that, good manners or not, Rupert had actually been quite offended when she'd sent him dinnerless on his way. Cassie sighed, all the exhilaration of the afternoon suddenly evaporated at the reminder that all her frenzy of organisation for the evening with Rupert, plus the money spent on her dress and hair, had been a total waste.

Cassie took her tea into the other room and curled up in her usual chair, explaining that this particular Saturday was fairly unusual. Meg and Hannah both had boyfriends who practically lived here, and the two men often brought other male friends along with them at weekends. Sometimes the entire household went out clubbing together, other Saturdays they sent out for a meal and talked into the small hours. Sometimes the visitors didn't even bother to go home, preferring to sleep on the sitting-room floor and stay to breakfast.

'Rupert,' she added, 'was the first man I've actually asked to a cosy little dinner for two.'

Nick watched her over his cup, the sea-blue eyes startling in his brown face. 'If I spoiled things for you, I'm sorry.'

'Are you?'

He shrugged. 'To be honest, no, I'm not. I think young Rupert's a bit lightweight. You need someone with more steel.'

Cassie's eyes narrowed angrily. 'You don't know a thing about me, Nick. Nor Rupert. You're in no position to make snap judgements.'

'You're right. It's none of my business,' he said shortly, and eyed the mountain of packages. 'If you'll provide me with a scissors, I'll get started. On the other hand,' he added, jumping to his feet, 'I can just leave you in peace and take this lot home to pack. I'll bring the finished articles round some time before you leave for Chastlecombe.'

'Oh, sit down again,' she said irritably. 'We've started so we may as well finish!'

To her surprise Cassie didn't want to be left in peace. Nick was right. She wasn't used to Saturdays on her own. What she hadn't told him was that, while some weekends were spent exactly as she'd described, other times she went home to Chastlecombe when Julia did, or spent the weekend in Acton, taking Emily for walks and helping with bathtime, even doing some ironing sometimes, while Julia cooked a meal. But she wasn't letting Nick Seymour know that. She much preferred him to picture every one of her weekends as a giddy social whirl from start to finish.

I wish! she thought in amusement, and looked up to find Nick watching her as he sealed a parcel.

'What now?' she demanded, passing over a vast gold bow for the finishing touch.

'I was just thinking how much you've changed since I saw you last.'

'Since last night, you mean? I just brushed all those silly ringlets out.'

He shook his head impatiently. 'I meant since Max and Julia parted.'

'Of course I've changed. I'm quite a bit older for a

start.' Cassie met his eyes head-on. 'And my sister's experience at Max Seymour's hands rather speeded up my maturing process.'

'Has Julia made you wary of relationships?' he asked curiously.

'Not Julia. Max. No way am I ever going to let any man ruin my life like that.' She smiled flippantly. 'Keep it light, that's my motto. Fun and good company, no strings.'

'No hankerings after marriage and children?'

'The two are not interdependent these days, Nick,' she informed him tartly. 'I like children, and I quite fancy one of them for myself one day. But a husband isn't necessary for that.'

Nick shook his head. 'My brother has more to answer for than I thought.'

'Maybe he's already answered for it.' She held her hand out for Paddington Bear. 'Have you faced the fact that he might not make it back this time?'

'Yes,' he said grimly. 'Of course I have. But Max is a tough customer. He can take care of himself. He's been late from his travels before. You know that.'

'Don't I just!' she declared, battling to wrap the toy in shiny paper. 'Julia spent a lot of sleepless nights right from the time she first worked for him, not just after they were married.'

Nick nodded morosely. 'Max doesn't deserve a woman like Julia.'

'But you do?' asked Cassie sweetly.

'That's not what I meant.' His eyes glittered angrily. 'Laugh if you want, but I'm fool enough to hope some-one will care for me like that one day.'

'My only surprise is that you haven't found the lady

already,' Cassie assured him, then surveyed the finished parcel with satisfaction. 'There, will that do?'

When the parcels were finished, Nick insisted on helping Cassie carry them up to her room.

'So this is your private retreat,' he said, looking round at her possessions.

'That's right. And before you ask, it's not the room Julia once occupied—though you probably knew that already, of course,' she added, holding the door open for him.

Nick gave her a dark, hostile look. 'As it happens, I didn't.' He turned abruptly and ran downstairs to take his jacket from one of the hall pegs. He looked at Cassie levelly as she went down to join him. 'Thanks for all the help. To show my appreciation I'll buy you dinner.'

But Cassie was shaking her head before the words left his mouth. 'No, thanks, Nick. I enjoyed the afternoon. And I'm very glad we've sorted Alice out for Christmas. But I won't come out for a meal with you.'

'You said you had nothing planned,' he reminded her.

'I don't. For once I'll have something on a tray in front of the television, or read a book. On my own—quite a novelty in this household.' She smiled politely and held out her hand. 'Thanks for taking me shopping. Have a good Christmas.'

Nick looked at the hand, but made no move to take it. His eyes moved back to her face. 'Tell me the real reason, Cassie.'

'What do you mean?'

'We had a good time together this afternoon, once the worries about Alice were over. We could do the same over a meal tonight.' He moved closer. 'Why spend the time alone here, while I do the same in Chiswick? What, exactly, do you have against joining forces, Cassie? Do you actively dislike me?'

'No.' She backed away a little. 'I don't. But you and I, Nick, have too much family angst hanging over us for comfort. Besides,' she added, looking him in the eye, 'I fancy my main attraction for you is my fleeting resemblance to Julia. So, thanks for the invitation, but no, thanks.'

Without moving a muscle, Dominic Seymour suddenly, and very visibly, lost his temper.

'Once and for all, I am *not* hankering after Julia,' he said between his teeth. 'All right, so I was in love with Julia for a brief time in my youth. But, like most attacks of puppy love, I got over it. Since that bloody awful afternoon I hadn't seen Julia until last night. I'm deeply sorry for her, but I am *not* in love with her.' Nick seized Cassie by her elbows, his fingers biting into her skin as his eyes bored into hers. 'Nor do I think you look the least like her!' Suddenly his hands dropped. 'You're shaking,' he said, taken aback.

'Is it any wonder?' she spat at him. 'You frightened me.' She rubbed her arms furiously. 'Go away and pick on someone your own size, Dominic Seymour.'

'I apologise,' he said tautly, something in his face telling her he was appalled by his lapse of control. 'Not for what I said. That was the truth. But I'm sorry for the bruises, Cassie. I've never hurt a woman physically before.'

'And you're not going to do it again with this one,' she retorted, furious with herself for letting him frighten her. She marched past him to the front door and flung it open. 'Goodbye.'

He reached round her and closed it again. 'It's not surprising I lost it just now, Cassie. You keep jerking my chain. The alternative was this.' And he yanked her into his arms and kissed her hard.

She gasped in surprise, which was a tactical error. Nick's tongue slid into her open mouth, the kiss suddenly fierce as he pulled her closer. For a split-second Cassie felt a surge of response. Then she came back to earth with a bump and shoved at him in a rage.

'I'm not going to apologise for that,' Nick informed her as his arms dropped away. He opened the door again, smiling down into her blazing eyes, and Cassie glared back, her face on fire.

'Get lost,' she snapped, in a voice she couldn't keep quite steady.

He shrugged, looking infuriatingly relaxed, as though the kiss had quenched the fury he'd burned with only a minute or two before. 'All right, Cassie, I'm going. Merry Christmas, by the way, and give my love to Alice. Will your parents mind if I ring her at your place over the holidays?'

'No. *They* won't,' said Cassie pointedly. 'Goodbye.'

She shut the door on him and went back into the sitting-room to sit staring into space for a while, then roused herself irritably and went to make herself something to eat. While she was toasting a cheese sandwich Cassie couldn't help a pang of regret for the meal she could have eaten with Nick in some expensive restaurant. But Nick Seymour was off-limits as a companion for a night out. From all points of view. She'd seen his face when he'd first caught sight of Julia the night before. It might not have been the look of love, exactly, but it had been a long way from indifference. Nick could say what he liked, but he still felt *something* for his brother's wife. Whatever it was. Cassie bit into her sandwich without enthusiasm, deciding it was best to steer clear of Dominic Seymour. His kiss had been quite an experience. In a class of its own, if she were honest. But getting involved with him would only complicate a situation which was quite difficult enough already.

Next morning, much to Cassie's surprise, Rupert rang and asked her out to lunch.

'I didn't ring too early in case you were having a lie-in. Sorry I was tied up yesterday,' he apologised, 'but my parents came up to do some Christmas shopping. It was late by the time they went back, and I had something on last night. Hope you didn't think I was being awkward about Friday night.'

'No,' fibbed Cassie brightly. She mopped at her newly washed, dripping hair with a towel. 'Of course not.'

Rupert asked to pick her up at noon, and Cassie wrote a hasty note for Polly, who always slept the morning away on Sundays, then made some tea and took it to her room, wishing Rupert had given her more notice. Her hair took time to dry properly, and while she blasted it at maximum heat with her hairdryer she made a mental review of her wardrobe, with the aim of both looking good and feeling warm. It wouldn't do to meet Rupert blue with cold, with contrasting red nose.

When Rupert arrived early, looking like an advertisement for the latest après-ski wear, Cassie was dressed in brown velvet jeans and shirt, topped with a heavy cream sweater, and her long brown winter overcoat. And under it all, for the first time, she was wearing a lace-trimmed thermal camisole her mother, ever the optimist, had put in her stocking the previous Christmas.

'You look stunning, Cassie,' said Rupert, handing her up into the immaculate Range Rover.

She thanked him, and pulled her tangerine wool beret

lower over the hair that had refused to dry completely. She'd be lucky to avoid pneumonia, she thought gloomily.

They ate lunch in a pub by the river, seated near a roaring fire in a room bright with holly and tinsel and lively fellow lunchers. But something was amiss. Rupert was a charming and attentive companion, but when he moved closer and took her hand Cassie felt embarrassed rather than thrilled. Either it was her thermal camisole or she was getting a temperature, she thought in dismay, and smiled up at Rupert with such determined warmth he moved closer.

'Actually, Cassie, there's something I want to say,' he began, looking down into her eyes.

'Yes?' she said faintly. Surely he wasn't getting any romantic ideas! Then it occurred to her that right up to Friday night any romantic idea on Rupert's part would have met with a delighted reception. Much money and effort had been spent with just that thought in view.

'The thing is, Cassie, I'm desperately sorry, but I can't give you a lift down to Gloucestershire on Christmas Eve after all,' he said contritely.

Deeply relieved, Cassie gave him a glowing smile. 'Not to worry,' she said cheerfully. 'I'll go on the train as usual.'

Rupert's eyes lit up. 'I say, Cassie, you really are a star. Any other girl would bawl me out for letting her down.'

Woman, not girl, she corrected silently. 'Don't worry about it, Rupert. I normally go down by train anyway. My father meets me in Cheltenham.'

'You're an angel. Let me get you a drink.' He jumped up with such blazing relief on his face Cassie couldn't help wondering about the other women in his life. He'd obviously expected a mega-tantrum.

'Just coffee, please,' she said, smiling, and sat back in her seat, passing a hand over the hair she'd anchored into a knot in preference to letting it fly about half-damp.

'The thing is,' said Rupert, when he got back with their coffee, 'my parents asked me to go home later this afternoon. Take Monday off. They're having a party tomorrow and want me there.'

'Why didn't you go back with them yesterday, then?' asked Cassie, surprised.

He looked embarrassed. 'I was meeting some of the blokes last night. Besides, I wanted to see you in person today, to explain. I couldn't just tell you over the phone.' He recaptured her hand. 'Cassie, when do you get back after the holidays?'

'On the twenty-seventh. Why?'

'I wondered if we could do something together on New Year's Eve.'

Cassie couldn't imagine why she didn't feel more excited at the prospect. She was obviously about to come down with some horrible virus. She would have to go to bed and stay there all over the holidays, with two children in the house. Or, worse still, stay home in Shepherd's Bush and spend Christmas alone with her germs. 'Actually, we're having a fancy dress party at the house for New Year's,' she said brightly. 'Would you like to join us, Rupert?'

'Would I!' he said, beaming. 'Thanks a lot, Cassie.'

After Rupert drove her home, Cassie joined Polly in the sitting-room for tea, refusing the crumpets she was offered.

'Big lunch,' she said absently.

'What's the matter?' demanded Polly. 'Didn't you have a good time with the delightful Rupert?'

'How did you know he's delightful?'

'I peeped round the curtain when he was kissing you goodbye on the pavement. Such a sweet little peck on the cheek.'

'Mmm,' said Cassie inattentively.

'Did the sexy Mr Seymour kiss you on the cheek too?' demanded Polly, and Cassie scowled.

'No, he didn't,' she said crossly. Which was true enough. 'Do shut up, Polly. I've just realised that now my lift to Chastlecombe's fallen through, I'm doomed to travelling with a sackload of presents on a packed train.'

'Did you forget to send the stuff with your father?'

'We hadn't bought any of it then.'

'We?' pounced Polly.

'I went shopping with Nick Seymour after you left yesterday. He's just got back from Saudi and asked me to lend a hand.' Cassie blew out her cheeks. 'Most of it was for Alice and Emily, so naturally I offered to deliver the presents for him.'

'Naturally. *I* wouldn't refuse him anything, either!'

Cassie scowled at her. 'Now I'll have to juggle with the stuff on the train.'

'If,' Polly pointed out, 'you're lucky enough to get on a train. They're probably all booked by this time.'

Cassie shot to her feet, groaning, and raced to the phone. When she rejoined Polly, after a long wait to get through to book a ticket, she nodded her head in depressed confirmation. 'If I go first thing tomorrow morning, fine. Otherwise not a chance. And I just can't leave the bank until tomorrow afternoon. Christmas or no Christmas.'

'How about the rest of your crew there? Are any of them heading for your neck of the woods?'

Cassie shook her head. 'I do know someone going in my direction,' she admitted reluctantly, 'but I'll only ask him as a last resort. And before you apply the thumbscrews, it's Nick Seymour.'

Polly's jaw dropped. 'I'm worried about you, Cass,' she said at last. 'You mean the sexy pirate's heading your way for Christmas and you won't ask him for a lift?'

'There are reasons,' said Cassie with dignity. 'We don't exactly top each other's list of favourite people.'

'Transfer him to mine and I'll give Jack the push, stat!'

'You don't mean that.'

'Don't be so sure.' Polly paused in the doorway, on her way to make more tea. 'If Nick Seymour's the answer to your problem, ducky, get on the phone and do some sweet talking.'

Cassie spent the evening arguing with herself. During her morning call home she'd learned that her father's elderly car had only just made it back with Julia and the girls. It was now in the garage for repair, which meant she couldn't ask him to come and fetch her. Not that she'd wanted to. He'd driven to London and back only yesterday. Her father was neither young nor immortal. The only alternative was a small fortune for a taxi. Only it wasn't the only alternative. At last, with Polly egging her on unmercifully, Cassie rang the Chiswick house.

'Dominic Seymour,' said a familiar voice, and Cassie leaned against the wall among the hanging overcoats.

'It's me, Nick,' she said gruffly. 'Cassie.'

'Why, hello,' he said after a pause. 'This is an unexpected pleasure.'

'I would have hung up if Max had answered. I suppose there's no news of him?'

'Afraid not. Is that why you rang?'

'No—'

'Is it Alice? Is something wrong?' he asked quickly.

'No, of course not. I spoke to Alice this morning. She's on top of the world, full of Julia and Emily and the dogs and so on. Her missing daddy is the only cloud in her sky.'

'That's good. Then why did you ring, Cassie? I'm delighted, of course—'

'I need a favour,' she said baldly, before she lost her nerve.

There was a nerve-stretching pause. 'Tell me what you want,' he said at last.

Cassie braced herself. 'This hotel you're going to,' she began. 'Is it very far from Chastlecombe?'

'Why?'

'I've got a problem. My lift has fallen through. My lift home for Christmas,' she added. 'Dad's car is in the garage, and I can't get a seat on a train after tomorrow morning. I must stay at the bank until early afternoon, at least, because some of the others are already on holiday. And I've got your presents to deliver.'

'Are you asking me for a lift, Cassie?'

What did he think she was doing? 'If it's not convenient, forget it,' she said huffily. 'I'll see if my father can drive up in my mother's car on Christmas Eve—'

'Hold your horses, Cassie,' he ordered. 'My reaction was astonishment, not reluctance. Of course I'll give you a lift. When do you want to go?'

'I'll fit in with your plans,' she assured him, trying hard to sound meek.

'What time will you leave work tomorrow?'

'Late afternoon some time, hopefully. Will that hold you up?'

'No. Just ring me when you get home and I'll come round and pick you up.'

'It's very kind of you,' she said stiffly. 'Thank you very much. By the way,' she added, 'what happens if Max turns up in the meantime?'

'If he does he can damn well make his own arrangements.'

Cassie sighed. 'If he turns up before Christmas, I suppose he'll rush Alice away from the Lovell household before you can say jingle bells.'

'No, he won't,' said Nick, very deliberately. 'As I told your father, I won't let anything spoil Alice's Christmas.'

In her relief at his solution to both problems Cassie thanked Nick with a lot more warmth than before. 'See you tomorrow, then.'

'I'll look forward to it, Cassie.'

CHAPTER FIVE

CASSIE got home later than she'd hoped next day, and it was after five by the time she rang Nick.

'Sorry I'm late,' she said breathlessly. 'I've run all the way from the Underground through a snow shower, would you believe? Quite heavy for London, too. Perhaps we'll have a white Christmas for once.'

'Let's hope it holds off until I get you safely delivered to Chastlecombe,' said Nick. 'I'm on my way.'

To mark the festive season, at the bank Cassie had worn a cream knitted suit with a tunic top and ankle-length side-slit skirt over her chestnut leather boots, and was ready to go as she was, barring a few repairs to her face. She put a gaily wrapped present on each of her friends' pillows, then stuffed the rest of her parcels into bin liners, collected her suitcases and hauled everything downstairs. With an eye on the clock, she gulped down a cup of coffee, then shrugged back into her overcoat and pulled her wool beret over her hair just as the doorbell rang.

'Hi, Cassie,' said Nick, clapping his gloved hands together as she opened the door. He wore a heavy rollneck sweater under his fleece-lined bomber jacket, and flakes of snow caught in his thick black hair as he stamped his booted feet to keep warm.

'You were quick. Coffee first?' she enquired, but he shook his head.

'If you're ready we'd better be on our way, before this lot decides to come down for real.'

'No Max, then?' said Cassie, as they stowed her belongings in the car.

'Nothing. I've made every enquiry I can think of through all the usual channels. So has his agent. But not a word, so far.' Nick glanced at her. 'I'll be frank with you, Cassie. I'm hellish worried.'

'If he's lost somewhere I imagine Max is worried, too. About Alice, if nothing else.'

The traffic was so heavy Nick made no more attempt at conversation until they were on the Chiswick fly-over. And as they headed out of London in thickening snow Cassie, no lover of motoring, was much reassured to find Nick was keeping meticulously to the minimum speed warnings flashing overhead.

'Before I went off to Saudi,' he said eventually, 'Max told me this trip to New Guinea would be the last time he'd be out of the UK for anything other than a holiday in future. He's been offered a chair in Anthropology at Cambridge, at his old university.'

Cassie whistled. 'Sounds good—' She halted abruptly. 'What about Alice?'

'Max isn't sure yet. If she's happy at her present school he may leave her there. If not, he'll take her with him to Cambridge and enrol her at a day school.'

'Behaving like a real father for a change,' said Cassie with asperity. She sighed. 'If he does take Alice from Broadmeads it means Mother and I won't be able to sneak her out to see Julia any more.'

'I won't see her much, either,' said Nick morosely. 'Max and I communicate a bit more lately. But I don't expect many invitations to Cambridge.'

'Perhaps he'll have had a change of heart by the time he gets back.'

'*If* he gets back.'

There was silence as they drove along in a solid stream of traffic heading out of London through worsening visibility.

'Heavens, Nick, I *am* sorry,' said Cassie with contrition. 'If it hadn't been for me you'd have avoided all this.'

He gave her a wry smile, and switched up the heater. 'Actually, I wasn't leaving until tomorrow, to give Max a chance to turn up. But when you called I could hardly refuse a maiden in distress.'

She stared at him in dismay. 'I should have asked Dad to fetch me in my mother's car.'

'In this?'

'No,' she admitted. 'I suppose not.'

'Look on the bright side,' said Nick. 'Tomorrow the weather might be worse, in which case I wouldn't have made it to the hotel at all.'

'You'll be lucky if you make it tonight!'

'The car's pretty reliable. Not as fancy as your pal Rupert's, but just as good in bad weather. Don't worry, Cassie. I'll get you home. When are your parents expecting you?'

'Not until tomorrow.' Cassie shrugged. 'I didn't know quite when we'd get there this evening, so I thought I'd just turn up and surprise them.'

'All to the good. At least they won't be worrying if we're a bit late.'

'I'm just a bit worried myself,' she admitted, as they slowed down to a crawl at one point. 'This weather's terrible.'

'Different from the desert, I grant you.' Nick gave her a sidelong grin. 'But I'm a brilliant driver, so have faith, Cassie.'

Despite his cheerful attitude, Cassie knew Nick

needed all his powers of concentration for the drive, without any unnecessary distraction from his jittery passenger. Nick was right, she thought with justice. He was a very good driver indeed. But Cassie was glad when they'd passed Reading and the traffic thinned out. When the snow showed signs of easing she relaxed slightly, and Nick shot a glance at her face.

'We should make better time now.'

'You don't have to hurry for me,' she assured him, alarmed.

'I won't break the speed limit,' he retorted, 'but at least we don't have to crawl any more.'

Cassie was not as comforted by this as she might have been, particularly when a car roaring past in the fast lane skidded spectacularly, and almost crashed into the central reservation before the driver regained control. With a glance at his passenger's petrified face, Nick moved over smoothly into the slow lane and stayed there, only moving from it when he was forced to overtake a heavy goods vehicle from time to time.

'Will we be turning off soon?' asked Cassie hopefully. 'Sorry to be such a coward, but I hate motorways.'

'They have their uses, but tonight I'm not fond of them myself,' he admitted. 'Sorry, Cassie, but we'd better stick to the M4 as long as possible tonight in this. We'll turn off before the Severn Bridge and go up north on the M5 for a bit, before we actually strike off across country.'

It seemed like hours to Cassie before they finally left the motorway, but once they had she soon discovered they'd merely exchanged one type of hazard for another. Their route lay along a major highway for a short distance, but the traffic was heavy, and, unlike the motorway, the road wound its way up and down through undulating countryside, the worsening snow rendering the road surface so treacherous it took all Nick's skill to keep the car from skidding.

'Are you all right?' said Nick at one stage, without taking his eyes from the road.

'Yes,' lied Cassie valiantly, secretly scared out of her wits.

Shortly afterwards Nick turned off on a minor road, which was even more winding, and a lot steeper in places, but less clogged with traffic. The snow was now approaching blizzard proportions, the rising wind hurling it against the windscreen with increasing force. And as the crowning touch they suddenly drove into a blank wall of freezing fog. Nick swore under his breath, leaning forward to peer through the windscreen as he slowed the car to a crawl.

'Pretty bad, isn't it?' said Cassie gruffly.

'It's not good. On my recent travels camels were the main hazard, not snow.'

At times headlights pierced the gloom as vehicles crawled past on the other side of the road, but mostly they were marooned in a blank, white, roaring world far removed from the city they'd left behind, and often it was almost impossible to tell if they were keeping to the road.

Eventually, as a particularly savage gust of wind tore the falling curtain of snow apart, their headlights shone through the fog onto a sign advertising a pedigree herd of cattle.

'Right,' said Nick, and inched the car into the farm gateway. 'I need a breather, Cassie,' he said, rotating his neck. 'My eyes are on fire.'

'I'm not surprised,' she said with sympathy. 'I wish I'd thought to bring a flask. I'd kill for a hot drink.'

Nick eyed the sign thoughtfully. 'I thought it was better to press on than stop at one of the motorway services. But now we have stopped let's go up to the farm and see what they can do for us. We're a fair way from Chastlecombe yet.'

'Great idea,' said Cassie with enthusiasm, her spirits rising as Nick nosed the car down the snow-covered rutted farm track. 'Perhaps the weather will let up later,' she said hopefully.

Cassie's heart sank as she saw that though the farmhouse was large, with several snow-covered cars parked in the yard, the building was in darkness. But when Nick knocked on the door it opened quickly, to an accompaniment of barking dogs, and Cassie watched anxiously as he spoke to a large male figure silhouetted in dim, welcoming light. After a quick exchange Nick slithered back to the car and opened her door.

'We're in luck,' he announced in triumph, and helped Cassie out, steadying her as her boots slipped in the snow. 'Come on.' He locked the car and yanked her towards the entrance, where a burly, smiling man welcomed them in and led them through a hall, festive with paperchains and holly, but with only an oil lamp for light. He ushered them into a small, candlelit room with blazing logs burning in a large stone fireplace.

'I'm Ted Bennett,' he announced.

Nick held out his hand. 'My name's Seymour. Nick. And this is Cassie—'

'You look frozen, my dear,' interrupted the farmer. 'I'm afraid this weather's played its usual trick, cut our electricity supply for the time being, but there's a good fire in here so you sit down close to it and thaw out while I put your coats to dry. My wife's in the kitchen.

I'll get her to make some tea for starters. Then we'll see what we can do about a meal.'

'What a wonderfully kind man,' said Cassie, when he'd gone. 'I didn't expect a meal.'

Nick stretched, and held his hands out to the flames. 'Now food's actually been mentioned I'm starving. I don't know about you, but I could eat a horse, saddle and all.'

Cassie took off her beret and ran a hand over her coiled hair. 'I'll pass on the saddle, but I'll fight you for the horse.'

Nick sat down beside her on a sofa drawn up to the fire. 'I don't mind telling you, Cassie, it was a bit hair-raising out there at times. I'm glad of a respite before we push on.'

'Perhaps the weather will ease a bit.'

'It can't get much worse!'

The door opened to admit a tall, thin teenager in jeans and a vast, baggy sweater, her red hair tied up with a ribbon with a sprig of holly stuck through it. She carried a loaded tray as if it was thistledown, and plonked it down on a small table near Cassie.

'Hi, I'm Tansy,' she said cheerfully. 'There's some biscuits to keep you going while Ma sorts your supper out. We've got a gas cooker, thank goodness. Terrible out there tonight; you were lucky to make it this far. Dad said you've come from London.'

'That's right. It was pretty terrifying for the last few miles,' said Cassie, smiling warmly. 'This is wonderful. Thank your mother very much indeed.'

'I hope we're not putting her out too much,' added Nick.

Tansy shook her red head. 'Ma's never put out. She'll be with you in a minute.'

Cassie could tell Nick was just as surprised as she was when 'Ma' proved to be a slender dark-haired woman in well-cut jeans and thick wool jersey.

'Hello. I'm Grace Bennett. Sorry I wasn't on hand to greet you. I gather you're orphans of the storm. A good thing you found us.'

'A very good thing,' said Nick fervently, as he shook her hand. 'I only hope we're not causing you too much trouble.'

Mrs Bennett shook her head briskly. 'Not at all. We're used to guests.'

Cassie smiled warmly. 'This is a wonderful house. How old is it?'

'Parts of it are seventeenth century—but not the plumbing,' said their hostess, eyes twinkling. 'Now to business. How do you feel about shepherd's pie?'

'Very enthusiastic!' said Nick with fervour.

'Right. Shan't be long. It'll soon heat up. There's a pile of daily papers on the table, and a few magazines.' With a friendly smile Grace Bennett took herself off, leaving two rather astonished guests behind her.

'What a charmer!' said Nick, as Cassie poured tea.

She grinned at him. 'She obviously bowled you over.'

'I'm a slave to any woman who offers me shepherd's pie,' Nick assured her, and accepted his tea with relish. 'We were lucky to chance on this place.'

'I'll say. Not everyone would be happy to welcome us in the middle of a power cut, especially so near Christmas.' Cassie sipped her tea ecstatically, eyeing her snow-stained leather boots. 'These are going to need some tender loving care when I can get to some polish.'

'Perhaps Father Christmas will bring you new ones.'

'These *are* new. I'll ask Tansy to lend me a pair of

wellies to get back into the car.' Cassie's face shadowed. 'Not that I'm looking forward to that part very much.'

'You'll feel better with some food inside you.' Nick gave her a leisurely sidelong survey, as Cassie leaned back in her corner of the sofa. 'You look very elegant. Is that how you dress for work?'

'No fear. Today I had lunch with the team to celebrate Christmas. Normally I keep to tailored suits.' Cassie began taking the pins from her neatly secured hair. 'These are driving me mad. But not even for a Christmas jolly would I wear my hair loose at the bank.'

'Why not?' he asked lazily, stretching like a big cat in the warmth from the fire.

'Mine is such frivolous hair.' She ran her fingers through the fair, rippling mass as it came loose. 'I've always longed for smooth, satiny stuff like Julia's—'

'Rubbish!' cut in Nick with unexpected force. 'Some women spend fortunes getting their hair to curl like yours. Though I agree it's a good move to pin it up during working hours.'

'Do you really?' she said with sarcasm.

His eyes gleamed as he put out a hand to touch one of the fair strands curling on her shoulder. 'For me, a woman's crowning glory is the ultimate turn-on. And I'm willing to bet this "team" of yours are with me to a man on the subject, Cassie.'

'You'd lose. Two of them are women.' She moved out of his reach. 'I pin my hair up to keep it out of my way, not to discourage carnal thoughts in my colleagues.'

'They've probably got those anyway,' he informed her, grinning lasciviously. 'As I've said before, Cassie, you've changed. I remember you as a teenager, thin as a whip, with hair cropped short like a boy. Now you're very definitely a woman. And a damned attractive one, at that.'

She eyed him mockingly. 'And you're a connoisseur of the breed, of course.'

'If you mean I like women, yes, I do.' Nick shrugged. 'What man doesn't?'

Cassie got up and collected some daily papers. 'Here,' she said, handing him one. 'Pull up a candle and let's catch up on the news. Otherwise we'll come to blows.'

'No, Cassie. No blows,' he returned with emphasis. 'If you're referring to my lapse into brute force the other night, you have my word it won't happen again.'

'Even though I have this knack of jerking your chain?'

Nick looked into her eyes for a long, silent interval, until Cassie's dropped, her face flushed with more than warmth from the flames. 'Even so,' he said very softly, and got up and added a couple of logs to the blaze.

For a while there was silence in the room as they both applied themselves assiduously to the daily news.

'It seems a white Christmas is pretty widely forecast this year,' said Nick after a while.

Cassie nodded glumly. 'A pity it couldn't have held off till we got home.'

'I've got to press on north of Worcester after that,' he remarked.

She stared at him, startled. 'I'd forgotten I was taking you that far out of your way.'

'If I'd been making straight for the hotel I'd have taken a different route.'

Why, thought Cassie, gazing at him with troubled eyes, does everything have to be so complicated?

'Don't worry, Cassie.' He took her hand. 'Don't look like that. I've said I'll get you home and I will. It may not be as soon as we'd hoped, but we'll get there some time.'

'Which reminds me,' she said thoughtfully, 'what happens when Max gets back to an empty house and finds his daughter missing?'

Nick's grasp tightened. 'I've left a note, informing him she's safe with your parents.'

'He won't take kindly to that!'

'Possibly not. But, as I told you before, I made my opinion very plain on the subject of spoiling Christmas for Alice. Or anyone else. If he really loves his daughter he'll take my advice for once.' Nick looked up with a smile and got to his feet as Ted Bennett came in with a loaded tray.

'Grace thought you'd like to eat in here,' said their host. 'You'd freeze in the dining-room.'

The grateful guests were soon consuming platefuls of savoury shepherd's pie with a potato crust enriched with cheese and leeks, accompanied by roast parsnips and buttered winter cabbage.

They ate in concentrated silence for a moment, with no attention to spare for anything other than the food.

'This,' said Nick indistinctly, 'is sublime.'

'Mmm,' agreed Cassie. 'Want some more?'

They shared the rest of the pie and finished off the vegetables, then Cassie stacked everything neatly on the tray and sat back with a sigh.

'My lunch was eaten a very long time ago. I really needed that.'

'Janet came in this morning, and provided me with a bowl of home-made soup and some bread she bought with the rest of the supplies she's left in the house for Max.' Nick shrugged. 'If he does make it at least he won't starve.'

Grace Bennet came in later, with coffee and a plate of mince pies. 'I made these this afternoon. I thought you'd prefer them to the remains of the family rice pudding.'

Nick sprang to take the tray from her. 'You're very kind, Mrs Bennett. The dinner was wonderful. Thank you.'

Cassie added her own thanks, feeling a pang of apprehension at the look on Mrs Bennett's face. 'Is something wrong?' she asked.

'I'm afraid I'm the bearer of bad tidings. One of Ted's farm hands just rang through to say the road up ahead is blocked. It catches the full force of the wind on the next rise and the snow's drifted to make it impassable for a while. Unfortunately he's the wizard who copes with our emergency generator, but I told him he mustn't even think of trying to get back here tonight, so we won't have any power until morning.' She looked from Nick to Cassie with sympathy. 'Were you desperate to get somewhere tonight?'

'We're not expected until tomorrow,' said Nick. 'So from that point of view we're all right.'

'That's fine, then. We can put you up here, and by tomorrow the road will probably be clear enough for you to go on,' said Mrs Bennett briskly. 'We cater for tourists regularly during the summer months, and often get one or two during the winter. Two pairs of grandparents are with us, which is why we had the fire lit ready in here, but the Aga in the kitchen is solid fuel, so they're perfectly happy out there with our young. I always keep one room for unexpected guests. I'll show you up to it when you're ready.'

There was a pregnant silence after their hostess left.

'One room,' said Cassie without inflection.

Nick nodded, eyeing her warily. 'I can always sneak down here later and sleep on the sofa.'

'You can't keep the fire blazing all night, and there's no heating, so you'd freeze.'

They looked at each other for a moment.

'I don't snore,' Nick assured her.

'I know.'

'How?'

'You slept on *my* sofa. I had the job of waking you up.' Cassie shrugged, and got up to pour coffee. 'We'll just have to make the best of it. Maybe the room has two beds.'

'Or a spare sofa,' said Nick, trying to keep a straight face.

'You may find it funny,' she retorted, handing his coffee over. 'I don't.'

'At least you can't accuse me of arranging all this,' he pointed out. 'The weather's beyond my control.'

'I know.' Cassie passed the mince pies. 'Funny, really. I'd expected to be driving down here with Rupert.'

'In which case, of course, the matter of the room wouldn't have been a problem!'

'I don't know. I've never shared a room with Rupert.'

Nick looked at her speculatively. 'What happened to the good-looking lad you always had in tow in the old days?'

Cassie took a mince pie and bit into it. 'Piers? After monopolising my spare time for years, he took off with someone else.'

'So he's responsible for your outlook on men!'

'No. That's down to Max.' Cassie shrugged. 'Not that I'm against every one of you—'

'Just Max and me, and the idiot you just mentioned.'

Nick reached out and touched her hair. 'He must have been crazy.'

Cassie moved out of reach. 'Let's not talk about him. Want some more coffee?'

With the prospect of sharing a room looming over her, Cassie found it very hard to relax, glad to be alone for a bit when Nick went out to bring in their bags. She replaced a couple of burnt-out candles and added more logs to the fire before he came back, teeth chattering and face pinched with cold beneath his rapidly fading tan.

'It's unbelievable out there!' he gasped. 'We were damn lucky to find this place, Cassie.'

She stirred the fire into a blaze. 'I know. Come and thaw out again.'

A knock was followed by Ted Bennett's face as he peered round the door. 'I heard you go out. Fancy a drop of mulled wine to restore circulation?'

They both accepted with gratitude, Cassie more concerned with easing her tension than improving her circulation.

'The Bennetts are very hospitable people,' said Nick, when they were alone. 'When I came across the hall I could hear roars of laughter from another room somewhere. A close-knit family, obviously.'

Cassie felt a sharp pang of homesickness for her own family, very glad she hadn't told them about her change of plan. At least they weren't worrying themselves to death about her. Then something occurred to her. 'Do you have your phone?'

'Yes. Why?'

'I've just had a thought. My mother might ring to ask what time I'm arriving tomorrow. And naturally Polly will tell her I've left already.'

'Hell, you're right.'

Mrs Lovell was pleased to hear from Cassie, as usual, and when she assumed her daughter was still in London Cassie decided to leave her in blissful ignorance of the facts. Ignoring the amusement in Nick's eyes, Cassie was deliberately vague about her time of arrival next day, asked about Alice and Emily and rang off. Then, at Nick's suggestion, she rang the house in Shepherd's Bush.

'What's the matter?' demanded Polly.

'If my mother rings say I'm in the bath, or something, and I'll ring back later, then ring me on this number.' Nick mouthed the number and Cassie repeated it to Polly, who was agog with curiosity.

'What are you up to, Cassie Lovell? Has your pirate made off with you, by any chance? Whose number is this?'

'I'll explain when I see you. Don't worry, I'm perfectly safe. Have a good Christmas.' Cassie rang off quickly, before Polly could fire any more questions at her.

'You're absolutely right, by the way,' said Nick, putting the phone away.

'What do you mean?'

'Despite indications to the contrary,' he said mockingly, 'you *are* perfectly safe. We may be forced to share a room, but with hand on my heart I swear I won't presume on my good fortune.'

CHAPTER SIX

TED BENNETT came in at that point, with a jug of steaming mulled wine and two glass tankards.

'This should do the trick,' he said jovially. 'I've taken your bags up, by the way. When you're ready just bang on the door where the noise is coming from. No television tonight, of course, so my youngsters conned me into giving them a glass of this stuff. They're a bit rowdy over some game they're playing, but don't worry, you won't hear them in your room.'

With Nick's words ringing in her ears, Cassie wanted to beg to join in the fun instead of going to bed. She cast a glance at the sofa when they were alone again, but Nick read her thoughts and shook his head, eyes gleaming.

'No, Cassie. If anyone sleeps on that it's me.'

'The logs are going down rapidly,' she pointed out. 'You'd be stiff with cold by morning.'

'So would you.' His eyes locked with hers. 'Look, Cassie, the weather's too cold for me to sleep in the car. So unless you want to beg a place in young Tansy's bed we'll just have to make the best of it. If our room boasts its own bathroom I can always sleep in the tub.'

Suddenly Cassie felt childish. She shook her head, and poured some hot wine into the tankards. 'I won't condemn you to that. Let's see the room first, before we start quarrelling about sleeping arrangements.'

'I don't blame you,' he said morosely. 'You've no cause to trust a Seymour.'

Cassie tasted the wine cautiously, then sipped with relish. 'This is gorgeous. Actually,' she added, trying to be fair, 'until the day Max started hurling accusations at Julia he made her very happy. Too jealous and possessive for my taste, but Julia had no problem with that. She loved him so much his attitude thrilled her.'

'He was a bloody fool to throw her out,' said Nick malevolently.

Cassie shook her head. 'Max didn't throw Julia out. She went of her own accord. Did a sort of U-turn. When he hurled accusations at her about the paternity of her baby something in Julia just snapped.'

Nick stared at Cassie in surprise. 'I had to leave for Nigeria that very day, so I never knew the actual details. It came as a shock to learn they'd split up, but I always assumed Max showed Julia the door like he did with me.'

Cassie shook her head. 'After the row Max shut himself in the study with a bottle of whisky. Alice was staying with her maternal grandmother at the time. So while Max was getting himself smashed Julia packed a bag and stole out of the house.'

'Did he try to follow her?'

'Of course he did. He went berserk later, when he found she'd gone. He chased down to Chastlecombe the minute he was sober, but Julia flatly refused to see him. He'd gone too far—committed the one sin she couldn't forgive.'

Nick whistled. 'I thought it was Max who wouldn't see Julia.'

'Is that what he said?'

'No. Max never tells me a thing.'

'When Julia refused to go back to him Max thought up the best revenge possible by forbidding to let her see

Alice. Which was such a bitter blow to Julia she can't forgive him for that, either. So she works herself to the bone, and Max takes himself as far away from her as he can get. And Alice pines for both of them.' Cassie shook her head. 'Though just between you and me, Dominic Seymour, I think she's frantic because he's missing. And not just for Alice's sake, either.'

'It's such a stupid, needless waste!' Nick sighed impatiently, and picked up the wine jug. 'Like some more of this? Our host was right. It does wonders for the circulation.'

'Just a spot. It may taste innocuous, but I bet it's got a kick like a mule.'

'I'll risk it.' He stretched out his long legs comfortably. 'I'm not driving anywhere tonight, so I might as well make the most of it. The drink, of course,' he added piously, and Cassie gave him a dark look.

'No need to hammer it home; I've got the message.'

They talked for a while, until the wine was gone and the fire was dying down. But the later it got the more Cassie's tension mounted. At last she couldn't bear it any longer, and got up, avoiding Nick's bright, comprehending eyes.

'These people probably get up at dawn. I'd better make a move.'

He jumped up to open the door for her. 'I'll give you a few minutes' start.'

'Thank you,' she said awkwardly.

There was no longer any noise coming from anywhere, and the only glimmer of light came from a door at the end of the long, shadowy hall. When Cassie knocked on it Grace Bennett appeared at once, with a torch, and took her up the shallow, worn oak stairs to the upper floor.

'This room's quite separate, in the oldest part of the house, so you'll be completely private.' She showed Cassie into a low-ceilinged room, with dark beams and red velvet curtains drawn over a window complete with padded seat in an embrasure in the thick stone wall. And there was just one double bed.

'There's a bathroom to yourself,' said Mrs Bennett, and moved round the room, lighting candles in strategic places. 'Not exactly self-contained, but it connects with your room, and the door to the landing bolts on the inside. Without any heating tonight I'm afraid it's cold in here. But I keep the bed aired.'

Cassie smiled at her gratefully. 'This is lovely. We were so lucky to find you. I can't thank you enough for taking us in.'

'My dear, it was no trouble. Breakfast is any time from seven on. Just shout when you get up and I'll send up a tray.'

Cassie sat down on a carved upright chair to remove her boots while she surveyed her quarters for the night. An armchair, a dressing table, a pair of wardrobes of dark carved wood like the bed, but no sofa. And the bathroom was lavishly provided with towels, and a dark red carpet like the bedroom, but the fittings were new and the bathtub more suited to her own proportions than Nick's. If anyone's going to sleep in the tub it had better be me, thought Cassie irritably, then shivered as a banshee howl from the wind outside changed her mind. This was silly. They were two sensible adults. The only problem was in her imagination.

By the time Nick tapped on the door later Cassie was in bed, the covers drawn up to her chin over her striped blue pyjamas, and she was trying to read a paperback novel by candlelight. He closed the door and stood against it, arms folded, his eyes taking in the room.

'No sofa,' said Cassie.

Nick's expression was hard to read in the flickering light. 'So I see.'

'But we do have a bathroom to ourselves,' she informed him, refusing to feel embarrassed. 'It's too cold to test the bathtub, but I can tell you now I'd have trouble sleeping in it myself, so not a hope for someone your size.'

'So what happens now?' he demanded, beginning to shiver. 'Hell, this room's like a deep freeze.'

'It's in the oldest part of the house. Mrs Bennett was so kind, and the room's so lovely, I hadn't the heart to say we weren't, well—'

'Lovers? Friends?'

Cassie looked at him mutinously. 'Whatever we are we're forced to share a room just this once, Dominic Seymour, out of sheer self-preservation. So get your kit off and come to bed. I'm tired.' It was the wine talking, she thought in horror, feeling the colour rush to her face.

Nick gave a snort of laughter as he pulled off his boots. 'That's the best offer I've had in a long time.'

'I didn't mean—'

'I know you didn't, Cassie.' He bent over her, and ruffled the fair curls. 'I'll take a candle to the bathroom to—er—get my kit off. I don't possess any pyjamas, so in the meantime you can snuff the other candles and I'll get into bed in the dark, so you're not shocked at the sight of my manly chest.'

Suddenly Cassie started to giggle. And having started couldn't stop.

'The wine was a mistake!' he commented. 'Quiet, woman. You'll wake the entire household.'

'I was just picturing Polly's face if she could see me now!' Cassie went off into gales of laughter again, pulling the quilt up to muffle her mirth. She came up for air, gasping. 'She fancies you madly, by the way.'

'Really,' said Nick, unamused.

Cassie nodded vigorously. 'She said if I didn't want you she'd gladly give her Jack the push and take over. I *think* she was joking.'

'Whether she was joking or not is purely academic,' he snapped. 'I'm not a can of beans on a supermarket shelf.' He grabbed his bag, marched into the bathroom with his candle, and, without actually slamming it, shut the door in a way which demonstrated his displeasure very graphically.

Cassie returned to her book, deflated, well aware that her laughter had been half hysteria because she felt so ill at ease. Which was stupid. She was a sensible adult, not a shrinking violet in a Victorian novel. And Nick was unlikely to get into bed stark naked. She was right. When he emerged he was attired in a large white T-shirt, a pair of navy boxer shorts and, as the finishing touch, white tennis socks which showed up the tan on his long legs.

'Cold feet?' she said, staring.

He nodded. 'Freezing.'

'Socks,' she told him, biting her lip, 'are quite a turn-off.'

He favoured her with a cold, blue stare, blew out his candle and got into bed. 'You were never turned on in the first place,' he said in the dark.

As a conversation-stopper his remark was effective. Cassie snuffed out her own candles, wriggled to the knife-edge of the bed and tried to compose herself for sleep, wishing now she'd asked Mrs Bennett for a hot water bottle. No doubt the lady had assumed sharing a bed with Nick would provide heat enough. But with a space as wide as the Grand Canyon between them Cassie grew colder by the minute. And as the temperature changed the floorboards began to creak, and timbers settled and shifted in the old house. Combined with the howling wind, the noises kept Cassie awake far more effectively than the traffic in Shepherd's Bush. It was no wonder she couldn't sleep, she told herself, trying to lie still. It was really nothing to do with the large, male presence in the bed. The only sound from Nick was quiet, even breathing, but Cassie grew steadily more conscious of it until it began to overtake the other night sounds in keeping her awake.

Get a grip, she scolded herself, then jumped violently as a quiet voice enquired whether she'd like to talk.

'Talk?' said Cassie, through chattering teeth.

Nick fumbled in the darkness, then struck a match, lit the candle on his bedside table and got out of bed to rummage in his bag. Cassie peered over the top of the quilt, as he pulled on a pair of thick jogging pants and a sweatshirt, got back in bed, propped up his pillows and sat upright.

'As you told me, you're not used to sharing a room,' he said conversationally. 'So I vote we talk until you feel more sleepy. Have you got a dressing-gown with you?'

Cassie nodded.

'Then put it on! Otherwise you'll never get to sleep. Seventeenth-century architecture may be picturesque, but it's hellish cold.'

Cassie leapt out of bed, rummaged in her bag, wrapped herself in her dressing-gown and dived back into bed to lie against the pillows Nick had piled ready for her.

'Sorry to keep you awake, Nick. It's all this creaking and groaning, not to mention the weather out there.'

'And the fact that I'm in the bed.' He laughed. 'It's quite funny, really. No one would believe us if we told them about this.'

'Certainly not Polly!' Cassie wriggled her icy toes. 'I don't suppose you'd have a spare pair of socks?'

He sighed, and got out of bed again to look in his bag. 'Anything to oblige.'

'Thank you,' said Cassie gratefully, and forced herself to put her legs out of bed to pull the socks on. 'Why all the sports gear?'

'The hotel boasts a squash court and a gym and so on.'

'I still find it strange that you're spending Christmas alone.' Cassie pulled the covers up again, shivering.

'Are you going to stop doing that soon?' asked Nick affably. 'You're letting in a stream of ice-cold air every time you move.'

'Sorry. I did my best to lie still before.'

'It was the corpse-like stillness that kept me awake.'

'Ungrateful pig! I was trying hard not to disturb you.'

'Without success. I was convinced you'd land on the floor any minute. Do you always sleep on the edge of the bed?'

'Only with strangers,' she retorted, and he smothered a laugh.

'Better now?' he asked, looking down at her.

'Much better. I don't know why I bothered to take any clothes off at all.'

'Tell me,' he said, sliding down lower under the covers. 'In these particular circumstances would you have been quite so tense and edgy if it were Rupert instead of me?'

Cassie thought about it at length. 'It's no good,' she said after a while. 'I just can't picture it.'

'You mean with you in pyjamas and dressing-gown, and Rupert almost fully dressed like me,' mocked Nick.

'Not in the least like you. Rupert's very image conscious. He'd probably be wearing silk pyjamas and a Noel Coward dressing-gown—and definitely no socks!' Cassie grinned up at him, pushing a rope of hair behind her ear.

He stared down at her, the laughter fading from his eyes, then without a word he slid out of bed.

'What are you doing now?' asked Cassie, bewildered.

Nick opened one of the wardrobes, took out an armful of blankets and flung them down on the carpet. 'Human nature being what it is, Cassandra Lovell, I'd better sleep on the floor. My intentions were—are—of the purest. But it just won't work.'

'You'll freeze!'

'Possibly. But I'll risk it.'

'We could roll the blankets up and make a sort of barrier down the middle of the bed,' she suggested, dismayed.

Nick straightened from his makeshift bed-arranging, and looked at her very explicitly. 'You would still be on the other side of it, Cassie. So throw me a pillow and blow out the candle.'

Without a word Cassie did as he said, and slid down in the bed in the dark, heart pounding. Nick was right, of course. He wasn't to blame. Nor was the mulled wine, though it had helped rather more than expected. The entire situation was fraught with risk. And not merely because Nick possessed all the usual male hormones and might want to make love to her. But because, for the first time in her life, she wasn't against the idea. Cassie stared into the darkness, remembering Nick's fierce, inflammatory kiss, and shivered with more than cold as she realised she no longer felt hostile towards him. She even wanted to believe him when he said he was no longer in love with Julia.

Cassie lay motionless for a time as she came to terms with the idea, but after a while grew even more aware of Nick's presence than when he'd been in the bed beside her. She heard him move restlessly on the creaking floorboards as he tried to get comfortable, and she began to worry in earnest as the room temperature dropped lower still. She was barely warm enough herself, in pyjamas and dressing-gown and Nick's socks, plus a generous topping of covers. She bit her lip in anxiety. After months in a hot climate he'd probably get pneumonia.

After a while Cassie could stand it no longer.

'Nick?'

'What?'

'I'm cold.'

'*You're* cold,' he said through chattering teeth.

'So if I'm cold you must be freezing,' she whispered urgently. 'Come into bed, for heaven's sake. I'll never get to sleep if you don't. Neither will you.'

There was silence for a while, then with a groan Nick got up in the dark, cursing under his breath as he tripped over his bag. He felt his way round the bed, thrust his pillow in place and got in, shivering violently. 'This is a bad idea,' he gasped.

'Better than the alternative,' she assured him.

'Which particular—alternative—are you—thinking of,' he asked with difficulty.

'Exposure, pneumonia—take your pick.' She reached

out for his hand, and he jumped as though she'd burnt him. 'You're like ice.'

'Tell me about it!'

'Turn around, away from me,' she ordered.

Nick complied without argument, and Cassie wriggled close against his back, put her arm round his waist, and tucked her knees behind his. 'Right,' she said imperiously. 'Lie still. Conserve your blood heat.'

There was silence as Nick's shivering diminished and his body gradually grew warmer. Eventually Cassie felt so comfortable pressed close to Nick's broad back she grew drowsy herself at last, as his body relaxed against her and he began to breathe deeply and regularly. At this point, she thought, some men might snore. Not Nick, though. She'd found that out already…

Cassie woke in the darkness, disorientated. Then she remembered where she was. And who she was with. Only now their positions were reversed. Nick was lying close behind her, one of his arms heavy round her waist. She lay motionless in the pitch-dark, afraid to breathe in case she disturbed him. And realised Nick was no longer asleep. He was perfectly still, breathing evenly, but he was definitely awake. And to her dismay Cassie found that a visit to the bathroom was imperative. She slid out of bed, shivering, and felt her way round the room in the darkness. Afterwards she picked her way back round the bed and slid in carefully, then found she was alone as the bathroom door clicked shut behind Nick.

Now for the tricky bit, she thought, biting her lip. Should she say nothing, pretend to be asleep? No. Nick would know she was faking. But under the present circumstances falling asleep quickly was impossible. For either of them.

Nick shut the bathroom door and stood by the bed.

'Oh, for heaven's sake get in,' she said crossly.

'It seemed only courteous to wait until invited.' He slid in beside her. 'The wind's dropped,' he whispered, as he lay at a discreet distance.

'Good.' Cassie buried her face in the pillow, trying to regain her former warmth, but this time she was the one shivering, and she clenched her teeth to stop them chattering.

'Cassie, come here,' Nick said briskly, and drew her against him, spoon fashion. 'There, you'll soon be warm. I speak from experience.'

'I bet you do.'

'I meant from earlier on, when you kindly brought me back to life.'

'Oh.'

'Go to sleep,' he ordered.

As if she could in these circumstances, thought Cassie bitterly.

'Do you want me to revert to the floor?' enquired Nick after a while.

'No.'

'Then for heaven's sake relax, woman!'

Cassie did her best to oblige, and eventually, as she grew warmer, some of the tension in her body decreased, and she wriggled slightly to get more comfortable.

'Be still!' ordered Nick gruffly.

Why, she thought in despair, does one immediately want to move about when told not to?

Suddenly Nick spun her round to face him, so that they were lying nose to nose in the darkness. 'Let's get this over, and then perhaps you'll get to sleep again.'

Cassie's heart lurched drunkenly in her chest. 'Get what over?'

'I'm going to give you a chaste kiss goodnight, then

we turn over and lie back to back for the rest of the night, awake or asleep, cold or not,' he said firmly. 'Agreed?'

'Would I dare do otherwise?' she said dryly.

Nick chuckled and ran a hand through her tousled curls, then bent his head to kiss her cheek. Cassie tensed, and suddenly he groaned and crushed her to him, putting an abrupt end to all the argument and skirmishing. As his hungry mouth closed over hers sudden heat transformed her shivering body into hot, fervent response. Skilled, caressing hands moved over her, pulling her close against the taut body that was warming as quickly as her own, and, heart hammering, blood coursing like fire through her veins, Cassie thrust her hands into Nick's hair and gave him back kiss for kiss. Then to her dismay he tore himself free, breathing in ragged gasps.

'Cassie, I can't—I must go. Now, while I can.'

'Don't go,' she whispered. 'Stay. Please.'

'If I do,' he panted, 'you know what will happen—*Cassie*' he said in despair, as she wriggled closer. 'I'm only human—'

'I know. So stop talking and make love to me.'

'Why, Cassie?' he demanded roughly. 'Why me?'

She turned her head away abruptly. 'If you don't want me, forget it—'

He dragged her chin round with an ungentle hand, his breathing rapid, in unison with hers. 'You know damn well I want you. I wanted to make love to you the moment I laid eyes on you last Friday night in that sexy dress. Thoughts of holding you in my arms kept distracting me even while I was driving through that damn blizzard tonight. Have you any idea how much self-control I've been exerting?'

'Too much,' said Cassie, utterly ravished by his confession, and with a muttered curse Nick held her cruelly tight.

'I'll probably regret this—'

'Afraid I won't respect you in the morning?'

The rash little challenge brought a soft, menacing growl from Nick, the fierce, renewed heat of his kisses like matches thrown on kindling. Cassie responded with total abandon, both of them rapidly so hot for each other the layers of clothes were pulled off with clumsy, feverish haste, and Nick gave a deep, relishing sigh as Cassie's naked body curved against his own. He buried his face in her hair, then tipped her face back and kissed her parted mouth, breathing in her breath as they shook in the throes of a desire so new and astonishing to Cassie her teeth chattered with heat instead of cold as Nick's hot, expert mouth moved down her throat to her breasts, his lips and grazing teeth sending streaks of fire through her entire body. She thrust herself against him with a demand which astonished her almost as much as it inflamed the man embracing her, but he drew in a deep, unsteady breath and held her still.

'First tell me why, Cassie,' he panted against her mouth.

'I'll tell you later.' Cassie thrust her face against his throat. 'Don't stop now. *Please.*' She revolved her hips against him in such shameless invitation Nick finally succumbed to the urges of his aroused body and granted her wish.

When, all too soon, it was over, Nick shot upright and lit the candle. Cassie put up a hand to hide her face, but he pulled it away, holding it fast. He stared down at her, still breathing raggedly, his eyes blazing with accusation as they met the guilt in hers.

CHAPTER SEVEN

'WHAT the hell were you playing at?' said Nick, incensed. 'You should have told me.'

Cassie shrugged defiantly. 'Was it so terrible, then?'

His jaw tightened. 'As you know perfectly well,' he said through his teeth, 'it was not. For me, anyway. But if I'd known—'

'That I was a beginner?' She looked away, hoping her heart would stop pounding soon. 'I dislike the term "virgin".'

'It's exactly what you were until a short time ago.' Nick pulled away. 'I'll collect our clothes before we start freezing again.'

'Making love certainly beats a hot water bottle,' she commented, flippant in her effort to sound normal.

'It ought to have been no comparison at all—nor would it have been if you'd enlightened me,' he snapped, and slid out of bed to retrieve the garments he'd scattered wide earlier on.

Cassie sat up and hauled the covers up under her chin, peering at Nick in the flickering light as he scooped their things into a bundle, then dived back into bed.

'If I'd told you I'd never made love before you'd have shot off to the sofa downstairs,' she said, wriggling into her pyjamas under the covers.

'Which is where I should have been from the start. Now the gesture's a bit superfluous. Besides, I want answers.'

'In the morning,' she pleaded.

'Not a chance. You're not going to sleep before I know one thing, at least,' he retorted. 'Why me, Cassie?'

She shrugged. 'Why not?'

'Stop it, Cassie,' he ordered. 'I want the truth.'

She slid down in the bed, and turned her head on the pillow to meet the dark-fringed eyes that no longer blazed with need but glittered in cold speculation. 'All right,' she began, as matter-of-factly as she could with a pulse-rate still far from normal, 'if you must know, I had a sort of crush on you once. When I was too young to know better. One day, I used to kid myself, Nick Seymour will look at me, discover I'm madly beautiful and fascinating, forget Julia, and carry me off on his big white horse.'

He stared at her, eyebrows raised, then smiled crookedly. 'Leave out the horse, and the rest isn't far out.'

Cassie scowled irritably. 'You really don't have to say that just to make me feel better.'

'So why do you think I jumped at the chance when you asked me to make love to you?' he demanded.

'Because you're a man, of course! What little I know about Arab countries, Dominic Seymour, leads me to assume you've had to do without the company of my sex for quite a while now.' Cassie shrugged. 'In the circumstances, human nature just took over.'

'So now we've established why *I* made love to *you*, animal that I am,' said Nick dryly, 'let's revert to your reasons.'

'I've told you—'

'No, you have not. Even if you did have a schoolgirl crush on me once, you're a big girl now, Cassie.' He grasped her hand. 'And pretty hostile most of the time, at that. You've made it very obvious that you don't have much time for me these days, due to reasons well known to both of us.' He frowned. 'But you had that steady boyfriend. Peter something.'

'Piers. He dumped me, remember?'

'Ah, yes. You said no to him and he took off in a huff.'

'Wrong. He said no to me.'

'What?' Nick stared at her incredulously. 'Are you joking?'

'It's not something to joke about!' she said crossly, trying to pull her hand away. 'I didn't find it remotely funny at the time. Nor is it common knowledge. I don't know why I mentioned it.'

'Because I asked,' he said tersely. 'Plus the fact that our present situation is a touch unusual.'

'If you mean it's made us do things we wouldn't normally do—'

'I don't mean that at all,' he retorted. 'The other part was bound to happen between us sooner or later, anyway.'

Cassie lay very still, her heart thumping so loudly she was sure Nick could hear it above the howl of the wind. 'What do you mean?' she said at last.

'Do I have to spell it out?'

'You bet you do!'

'I admit I was a touch heavy-handed last Friday, barging into your place after Alice, but I'm very glad I did.' Nick smiled at her, his teeth glinting white above the growth of black stubble along his tanned jaw. 'The warfare between our respective siblings had ruled out contact between us these past couple of years, so I suppose I still thought of you as little more than a schoolgirl—'

'If you thought of me at all,' muttered Cassie.

'Did you think of me much?' he said swiftly.

'Not recently, no. I used to languish over you when I

was too young to know better, it's true. But mainly because you wore your hair in a ponytail and sported designer stubble and a gold ring in your ear,' said Cassie, eyeing him objectively. 'You look more conventional these days. Pirate king turned sober engineer. Though the stubble's still there.'

'What do you expect at this hour?' Nick looked at her in silence. 'Look, Cassie, I admit that on Friday I fully expected to find Julia—'

'Don't I know it!'

'Instead,' he went on, ignoring her, 'I discovered a furious, gorgeous creature who took my breath away. Cassandra grown up and dressed to kill—'

'And about to entertain a friend,' she reminded him.

'True,' he agreed, unrepentant. 'Though I did you a favour by nipping *that* little romance in the bud.'

'You didn't, as it happens. I'm seeing Rupert on New Year's Eve.'

Nick propped himself up on the pillow and glared down at her. 'Then why the hell did you plead with *me* to make love to you just now? If it was some experiment you were making couldn't you have waited until Rupert was available?'

Cassie stared back defiantly. 'In the circumstances it seemed too good an opportunity to pass up—to prove something.'

There was a short, unfriendly pause.

'Explain,' said Nick coldly.

Cassie was silent for a moment, then let out a long, unsteady sigh. 'All right. But I've never told anybody this. You'll have to make allowances.'

Nick slid down again and pulled up the covers. 'Nothing you tell me will go any further, Cassie, on my honour. And, contrary to your belief, I *do* have some.'

She turned towards him impulsively. 'Don't be angry with me, please. There's no real harm done.'

'It depends on your point of view!'

'In fact,' she went on with determination, 'it did me a great deal of good.'

'Not as much as it could have,' he said bluntly. 'In full knowledge of the facts, I could have been less—precipitate. But you were irresistible, Cassie. I pride myself on my control in such matters as a rule, but—'

'I didn't mean that!' snapped Cassie, hoping he couldn't see she was blushing.

'Then tell me what the blazes you do mean,' he snapped. 'It's embarrassingly obvious that I can't get to sleep with you in the bed, so tell me a story instead, Scheherazade. Dawn is a long way away.' Nick reached up and blew out the candle. 'Perhaps darkness will make it easier.' He recaptured her hand and gave it an encouraging squeeze. 'Go on, Cassie. I'm listening.'

'Oh, all right.' She took in a deep breath. 'To go back to the start of it all, Piers and I went to single-sex schools which socialised occasionally, though my friends could never understand why I got on so well with him. Piers was very good-looking, and frighteningly clever, but a total loner before he met me.'

'And you changed things for him?'

'Yes. His parents pressurised him unmercifully, but with me Piers could just relax. Out of school hours he monopolised all my time from the moment we met. My parents worried about it, thought I should be having fun with lots of people my own age, not just one. Then Piers got a scholarship to Oxford, and I passed enough exams to get into my college. A couple of years later, there was all the excitement of Julia's wedding to Max. And you were there—brooding about the place like Heathcliff because Julia was marrying your brother.'

'I brought a girlfriend to the wedding,' he reminded her.

'I remember. Her cleavage, anyway.'

He laughed. 'My taste inclined to the obvious in those days.'

'Except for Julia.'

'We were discussing Piers,' he reminded her.

'Right. After Piers and I went our different educational ways we still saw each other a lot in vacations. His parents encouraged this.'

'Didn't they see you as a threat to his ultimate goal, whatever it was?'

'Quite the reverse. Piers's parents saw me as a socially acceptable girlfriend for their brilliant son,' said Cassie acidly.

In the summer of his final year at Oxford Piers had invited Cassie to the May Ball at his college. With the promise of a satin ballgown as encouragement, Cassie grew her hair into the long, tousled mane fashionable that summer, then set off for Oxford, full of anticipation.

'I had a wonderful time, though Piers was taken aback at my new image. I'd grown my hair long and my shape was a lot more girly by that time, which was a good thing, because my dress was strapless. Piers had changed, too. He had some pretty wild friends. Anyway, I had the time of my life, dancing with them all in turn. Then in the small hours Piers took me back to his room. By that stage I was dazzled with the glamour of it all, and fully expected Piers to whisk me into bed and make love to me for the first time to round off the evening.'

'So what happened?'

'He sat me down in a chair and explained that, while

he'd always be very fond of me as a friend, he'd recently fallen passionately, physically in love with someone else.'

Nick said something short and to the point. 'One of his fellow students?'

'Yes. Piers even wanted to introduce me, but I drew the line at that.'

'So why didn't the prat cancel your invitation?' demanded Nick.

'He felt he couldn't possibly hurt a "dear friend" like me by putting me off.'

'And hurt you far more by the idea that you weren't sexy enough to take to bed?'

'Right,' agreed Cassie. 'My vanity took a terrible beating. I was in a right old state, especially when it dawned on me that Piers's real reason for letting me turn up was to avoid wrath from his parents. He was lucky—they were furious with me instead, because I told everyone I'd dumped their beloved son.'

'Good move.'

She sighed gloomily. 'Piers turned me off men pretty conclusively. I've had boyfriends since then, of course, but with the accent on the friend bit—nothing heavy. Then Rupert came on the scene, and for the first time I was sure it would be different.'

'So last Friday night you were actually going to take the plunge at last,' said Nick slowly. 'I hadn't realised the occasion was quite so significant.'

'Neither had Rupert. Nor the others in the house. My status is a deadly secret. To be honest,' she added, chuckling, 'they think I've got a man I sneak off to see now and then at weekends.'

'Oh, yes? Where *do* you go?' he demanded.

'Home sometimes, or to Julia's, to change nappies and

play with Emily. But the others are sure I've got a married lover somewhere. So snitch on me and you die!'

Nick smothered a laugh, then fell silent for some time. 'Cassie,' he said at last, 'did you really ask me to make love to you just to see if I wanted you?'

'Yes,' she admitted honestly, omitting the fact that she'd have courted pneumonia on the sofa downstairs rather than share the bed with any other man. Rupert included, she realised, depressed. 'Though I'm sure you could tell I wasn't exactly averse to the idea myself, Nick, once you—er—'

'Displayed the necessary enthusiasm?' He gave an impatient sigh. 'As I said before, I've had to fight to keep my hands off you every minute we've spent together since last Friday. And,' he added, 'I can't be the only man you've affected that way, either.'

'No,' she admitted. 'But I could never bring myself to get this far before.'

'To avoid any possibility of rejection?'

'I've never thought of it like that, but you could be right,' she agreed, frowning.

'This brilliantly clever Piers of yours was a fool to prefer someone else,' said Nick savagely, and raised the hand he held to his lips, kissing each finger one by one in the flickering candlelight. Then he turned his head on the pillow to look at her. 'To rid you of any last doubts where I'm concerned, Cassandra Lovell, I want you so badly right now it's taking every last ounce of willpower I possess to keep my distance.'

Cassie lay very still, transfixed by the blue eyes locked with hers.

'If you want, I'll turn over and keep to my side of the bed and never move a muscle,' said Nick hoarsely.

'I'll get cold again,' she whispered, and he let out a

deep, ragged breath and pulled her into his arms and kissed her with a hunger Cassie shared with joy, delighting in the way Nick's breath caught as his body tensed under her caressing hands.

'Now,' he whispered against her parted lips, 'I'm going to teach you a whole lot more about lovemaking than I achieved earlier on. I hurt you, darling, didn't I?'

She nodded in the darkness, breathless at the endearment. 'I expected that.'

'It's not mandatory, Cassie. This time will be different.'

Cassie soon discovered he was right. By the time Nick finally consummated their lovemaking she was out of her mind with longing, every inch of her body clamorous in response to the expert mouth and hands that performed such exquisite torture she was panting and breathless, uttering stifled cries of entreaty Nick responded to at long last by taking her on a wild, heart-stopping race she won before him, her eyes wide with astonishment in the darkness, before she felt his body convulse with the same inexorable rapture as he held her so fiercely she thought her ribs would crack. And didn't care if they did.

They were still locked in each other's arms when an onslaught of creaking and groaning heralded the welcome return of the heating early next morning. Cassie stirred, Nick muttered something and tightened his grasp, and she sank back into sleep. When she woke again cold white light was sifting through a crack in the curtains, and there were sounds of activity outside.

Nick raised his head and looked into Cassie's heavy eyes. 'Good morning,' he whispered.

Her eyes fell. 'Good morning,' she whispered back, wondering what to do next.

He freed an arm to look at his watch. 'Hell, it's after eight.' He dropped a swift kiss on her mouth, then leapt out of bed and raced to the bathroom.

Cassie stared after him, lying very still as she went over the events of the night. In one way she had no regrets. She'd made her first essay into the art of love with an expert in the field. But Nick Seymour was a man who could cause havoc with her life if she wasn't careful. She'd recovered from her teenage crush on him with lightning speed when he was the cause of Julia's separation from Max, and since then she'd looked on him as the enemy. Now that was all changed by the freak of nature which had marooned them together for a night. An unforgettable night. But she couldn't blame Nick. In the circumstances any man worth his salt would have accepted her challenge. But then, she would never have got into bed with any other man, let alone pleaded with him to make love to her. Nor was Nick just any man. He was still, technically, her sister's brother-in-law. The fact that making love with him had been magical was irrelevant. Nick was Max Seymour's brother.

'Right, your turn,' said Nick, coming out of the bathroom. Fully dressed, newly shaved, his damp hair tidier than usual, the thickly fringed eyes smiling at her with a new, intimate warmth, he was hard to resist. But when he bent to kiss her, she turned her head away. 'Shy?' he teased.

'You've brushed your teeth,' she muttered. 'I haven't.'

'Then get a move on.' He went over to the window and drew back the curtains on a white world gleaming with pale sunlight. 'It's stopped snowing. I'll go down and see if there's any news—and order breakfast. I'm starving.'

Cassie was grateful for the return of electricity, which granted her a hot bath. Afterwards she took time to make up her face, embarrassed to find that it was tender from contact with the stubble she'd once thought so cool. By the time Nick came back she was dressed in a thick shirt under a canary-yellow sweater, and elderly fawn cords, her hair loose on her shoulders but reasonably tame. Unlike her heart, which thumped at the sight of him.

'Any news?' she asked coolly, packing her wool suit away.

'One of Ted Bennett's men came in early and got the emergency generator going. Snow ploughs have been out clearing the road, but we're advised to wait for an hour or two until gritters make the surface safe.' Nick leaned against the door, eyeing her searchingly. 'How are you, Cassie? Really?'

'I'm just fine,' she assured him.

'You look tired.'

'So do you.'

'You know what I want most right now?' he asked, moving from the door.

'No,' she said warily.

'I'd like to take you back to bed and sleep for hours and hours. Just sleep, Cassie,' he added as she backed away, relief in her eyes as a knock on the door heralded Tansy with the breakfast tray.

Cassie was embarrassed to find she was just as hungry as Nick, and made short work of a bowl of porridge before Tansy returned with a platter of bacon, eggs and sausages, with a promise of more toast later when it was ready.

'There is nothing in the world like the great British

breakfast,' said Nick with relish. 'I miss it when I'm abroad.'

'Would you eat this every day if you could?' asked Cassie, determinedly conversational.

'No. But I like to feel I can if I want.'

She looked at him curiously. 'Do you cook for yourself in this flat of yours, or does someone do it for you?'

Nick buttered a piece of toast. 'You mean do I have a girlfriend who rustles up a cordon bleu meal when I snap my fingers?'

'In your dreams, maybe,' she retorted.

'My dreams about women, Cassie, don't feature bacon and eggs,' he assured her suavely. 'And women in my past demanded meals in restaurants. If any of them could cook I never discovered it.' He smiled at her. 'Even you buy dinner from a food hall.'

'Only to impress *special* visitors,' Cassie informed him sweetly. 'I can cook simple meals. But I'm not in my mother's class. Or Julia's.'

'It's strange that someone who looks like Julia is so domesticated,' he commented, shaking his head. 'Max must be raving mad.' He looked at her soberly. 'While you were in the bath I rang the Chiswick house, and Max's agent, but still no news. It doesn't look good.'

'No, it doesn't,' said Cassie, ashamed to find she hadn't given Max a thought for some time. 'If—if the worst happens,' she went on with difficulty, 'are you Alice's guardian?'

'Yes.' Nick's mouth twisted. 'Much to my astonishment, Max asked me before he left this time. Don't worry. *I* won't keep Alice away from Julia.'

Of course he wouldn't, thought Cassie, It would be a golden opportunity to see Julia as much as he liked.

Nick reached across the small table and raised her face

with an ungentle finger. 'I can read you like a book,' he said with quiet menace. 'You're wrong. If you hadn't been convinced of it before last night, surely you are now?'

Cassie moved out of reach. 'Last night was an accident, Nick. It was something neither of us could have foreseen—'

'Which is beside the point,' he interrupted with force. 'If it hadn't happened last night, it would have happened some other night, or day, soon. Believe me.'

'Sorry. I don't.' Cassie pushed her plate away and poured coffee. 'I know you're trying to make me feel better about it, but you don't have to. There's no obligation on your part just because you were the first. To make love to me, I mean. It doesn't hold you—or me—to anything.' She gulped some coffee quickly.

Nick's eyes glittered dangerously, but to Cassie's relief Tansy interrupted with a fresh supply of toast to ask if they needed anything else.

'Mum says there's a nice fire in the little parlour when you want to go down,' she said, as she collected plates. 'Two more of Dad's men just got here. They said it's a bit dangerous up ahead yet, so best to hang on for a while. Should be all right in about an hour, though, with your sort of car.'

They thanked her, then Nick sat down again and helped himself to some toast. 'You have some too, Cassie. It might be a long time before we manage another meal.'

'I hope not,' she said glumly.

'You mean your family will worry if you're late,' he said, and held out his cup for more coffee. 'Personally, I'd be quite happy to stay where I am, in present company, right over Christmas—and I don't mean just because it was so good between us last night. Though it was, Cassie.' His eyes lit with a heat which contracted her stomach muscles. 'Something way outside my experience.'

'Well, it would be, wouldn't it?' she said tartly, and buttered a piece of toast she didn't want.

'I didn't mean that,' he said angrily, leaning towards her. 'What I'm trying to say, Cassandra Lovell, is that, ravishing though last night was, I'm equally happy sitting here sharing breakfast with you.'

Cassie gazed at him in silence, wishing vainly that he was anyone but Max Seymour's brother.

Nick waited expectantly, but when she said nothing his face hardened and he got to his feet. 'Come on, then, Cassie,' he said coldly. 'I'll take our bags down, then we'll sit by the fire in the parlour and read the papers.'

She shook her head. 'I doubt there'll be any.'

'Then we'll read yesterday's papers.'

When they went downstairs Grace Bennett was waiting in the hall. 'Not that we want to get rid of you,' she said, smiling, 'but I know you must be trying to get somewhere for Christmas. My lot have gone tobogganing, so they'll come and tell us when they see traffic getting through.'

An hour later, just as predicted, they were able to get on their way.

'It was very good of you to put us up last night, especially at this time of the year,' said Cassie gratefully, as they said their goodbyes to the Bennetts.

'Isn't that what Christmas is all about?' said Ted Bennett, shaking her hand. 'Only too glad to help out, Mrs Seymour. Come and stay with us again some time.'

'Preferably when it's warmer,' added his wife. 'Sorry

we had to give you the coldest room in the house, but it's the only one we keep on visitor alert.'

'We weren't cold,' Nick assured her.

'Why did Mr Bennett think I was your wife?' demanded Cassie later, as Nick negotiated the rutted, snow-covered track.

'Does it matter?' He shrugged. 'When I was settling up he assumed it, so I didn't bother to contradict him.'

'Which reminds me,' she said quickly. 'I'll go halves on whatever you had to pay.'

Nick favoured her with a cold blue glare. 'You will not!'

When they emerged from the farm track they found banks of snow piled high over the hedgerows. The road itself was gritted enough to make it passable, but only with extreme care. After driving slowly for a couple of miles Nick whistled as they passed more than one car abandoned at the side of the road.

'Our guardian angels were working well last night. Other people weren't so lucky.'

Cassie shivered. 'It's a good thing you spotted the Bennetts' sign.'

'So you're not sorry we were forced to spend the night together?' he demanded.

'No, I'm not.'

'From any point of view?'

She cast a look at his profile, her eyes objective on the thick black hair, the wide, resolute mouth and the dark-lashed blue eyes fixed on the road ahead. 'All right,' she said matter-of-factly. 'Let's mention it this once, then put it behind us, Nick. For me it had to happen some time, and you made it an experience I can look back on with pleasure. But that's all there is to it.'

Nick let out a snort of laughter, and she glared at him, offended.

'What's so funny?'

'You, Cassie. If you think I'm going to let things rest there between us, you're mistaken. I know where you live, remember.'

'Is that a threat?'

'Look on it more as a promise, Cassie.'

CHAPTER EIGHT

ALTHOUGH the road had been partially cleared all the way, it was still hazardous enough in places to add an hour to their journey. When they finally reached the steep main street of Chastlecombe Nick caught Cassie's eye and smiled.

'There. Almost home. Better now?'

Cassie nodded gratefully, and let out a sigh of relief as they approached the medieval arches of Chastlecombe market hall. Like the vast Christmas tree in the cobbled square, and all the crowded shops in the town, the arches were strung with lights and decorations, and with a layer of snow as literal icing on the cake the entire town looked like a Christmas card illustration. But to Cassie it was sanctuary.

'Thanks a lot, Nick. The only hurdle left now is the drive up to the house.'

The Lovells lived in an Edwardian house at the end of Ashdown Lane on the far side of town, an unadopted road with too few houses to merit the attention of a snow plough. After bumping along the ridged surface of the road, it took Nick every last scrap of skill he possessed to manoeuvre the vehicle up the steep, snow-covered bends of the drive to the terrace in front of the house. When they came to a halt he released his belt and blew his cheeks out.

'Right, Cassie, we made it.'

But Cassie was already out of the car, slipping and sliding up the path to the garlanded front door. It opened to let Alice out like a bullet from a gun as she raced to Cassie for a kiss and a hug before careering down the steps into her uncle's outstretched arms.

'Uncle Nick, did you bring Daddy?' she cried hopefully.

'Not yet, sweetheart. But he'll come soon.'

Alice struggled manfully with disappointment, and tugged at Nick's hand to lead him towards the open door, where the senior Lovells were hugging their younger daughter.

'Hello, Nick,' said Bill Lovell, holding out his hand. 'Cassie tells me you volunteered to get her here through this lot. I'm damned grateful to you. We were worried she'd be stuck in London. Couldn't ring to find out; the telephone's dead. My wife's been frantic. Come in quickly, and get warm.'

Charlotte Lovell, an older version of Julia, added her fervent thanks. 'Julia's getting Emily up from her nap. Come into the warm, Nick. You're just in time for a snack lunch.'

'That's very good of you,' he said quickly, 'but I ought to press on while I can. The weather doesn't look too good—'

'Oh, please stay for a bit,' pleaded Alice, clinging to his hand.

'You can spare an hour for a meal, Nick,' said Cassie briskly, and opened the kitchen door to a boisterous welcome from a pair of black retrievers. 'Hello, boys—*down*. Yes, I'm glad to see you, too. Leave Nick alone, you idiots—and stop licking Alice.'

The Lovell kitchen was a welcoming room, full of savoury aromas, with a big square table and rush-seated chairs. A vast dresser filled one entire wall, and windows on two sides gave breathtaking views of the garden and rolling hills beyond. And Cassie had never been so glad to see it in her entire life.

Bill Lovell took their coats, and his wife quickly laid extra places while she listened to Cassie's account of her adventure with Nick.

'I'm glad I didn't know you were out in that,' said her mother with a shudder. 'You were so fortunate to find shelter for the night.'

Cassie nodded, avoiding Nick's eye. 'Fortunately the Bennetts are geared up for tourists all year round.'

'Lucky for you,' said her father, opening a bottle of wine. 'On the news last night it said most minor roads in the county were blocked. Have some of this, Nick, while we wait for Julia and the baby.'

'Just half a glass, please. I've still got quite a way to go.'

'In this weather? Where are you bound?'

'A hotel north of Worcester.'

'You're spending Christmas at a *hotel*?' said Charlotte in disapproval.

'Yes. I did the same last year, so I booked early before I left for Riyadh,' said Nick, pulling Alice on his knee. 'Which reminds me. Thank you very much indeed for inviting this young lady for Christmas.'

'Our pleasure,' said Charlotte with emphasis. 'We're only too delighted to have her.'

'There's a big Christmas tree in the drawing-room, with presents under it, Uncle Nick,' said Alice excitedly. 'Come and see it—'

'After lunch,' said Charlotte firmly, and tousled the chestnut curls affectionately. 'Go and hurry Julia up, darling. Tell her Nick and Cassie are here.'

'So there's no news?' said Bill gravely, once Alice had run off.

Nick shook his head. 'I rang the house this morning, but Max hadn't arrived. I'll ring again before I set off.'

Cassie busied herself with cutting hunks off a crusty French loaf, assuring her mother that soup and bread and cheese would do very well. 'We had a vast breakfast at the farm.'

'A change from your usual slice of toast, then. Not,' added her mother, 'that you probably eat even that in London, without me to nag.'

'Of course I do,' fibbed Cassie unconvincingly.

'I can assure you she ate like a horse this morning, Mrs Lovell,' said Nick, his eyes glinting as he smiled at Cassie.

'I was hungry,' she retorted. 'Who wouldn't be in this weather?'

Nick jumped to his feet as the door opened and Alice came in, leading Emily by the hand. The toddler halted, startled at the sight of a stranger, then her face lit up under the chestnut curls.

'Hello, Cassie!' she said happily.

Cassie swept her up in her arms as Julia came in, nuzzling Emily's cheek as she watched Nick greet her sister. But even to Cassie's prejudiced eye there was nothing in his manner other than normal courtesy.

'Hello, there, Nick. Alice has been telling me all about your adventure in the snow.' Julia's eyes widened on his questioningly. When he shook his head Julia turned away sharply. 'You were lucky to find shelter, Cassie,' she said brightly, giving her a hug. 'Thank goodness we didn't know you were driving through all that snow.'

'I was scared stiff,' admitted Cassie, inserting Emily into her highchair. 'But Nick's a great driver. How he kept the car on the road at times I'll never know. When we pushed on this morning we saw quite a few vehicles abandoned by the roadside.'

Alice gazed at her, round-eyed. 'Did the people sleep in the cars?'

'I expect they walked the rest of the way,' said Cassie cheerfully. 'Where are you going to sit, poppet?'

Alice chose a seat between Cassie and Nick, where she could face Julia and Emily across the table. 'I have dinner at night here,' she said with satisfaction. 'Charlotte lets me stay up.'

Mrs Lovell ladled thick vegetable soup into bowls, smiling at Nick. 'I hope it's not against the rules.'

'I imagine all visitors are happy to abide by the rules of this house,' he said quickly, as she set a soup bowl in front of him. 'This smells wonderful. I've been eating remarkably well since I got back to the UK. Cassie gave me a fantastic meal last Friday once we knew Alice was safe.'

Three pairs of Lovell eyes turned on Cassie in surprise.

'I bought it ready-prepared,' she said defensively. 'I just had to read the instructions.'

Her father laughed as he handed Nick a dish of grated cheese. 'I pity the man our Cassandra marries.'

'I don't,' said Nick, and there was a sudden little silence, which Mrs Lovell broke by helping him to a second serving of soup, asking if he'd managed to do any Christmas shopping. She shot a surprised look at her younger daughter when Nick revealed that Cassie had accompanied him as adviser during the raid on Harrods.

'I thought you didn't care much for Nick Seymour,' said Charlotte Lovell later, after the men went with Alice and Emily to view the Christmas tree.

'I made the mistake of tarring him with the same

brush as Max,' said Cassie, and cast an apologetic glance at Julia's stricken face. 'Sorry, but it's the truth.'

'I just wish there was some news of him,' said her sister, and wiped the tray of her daughter's highchair with unnecessary force. 'Whatever else you can say about Max, he loves Alice.'

'So much he keeps her away from you!' retorted Cassie.

'Let's not get into all that,' commanded her mother. 'This is Christmas. Good will to all men. Even Max Seymour.'

Cassie nodded meekly. 'Whatever you say, Mother dear.'

'Then make some coffee while I put these away. Julia, go and find the others, tell them coffee in ten minutes in the kitchen.'

'Why ten minutes?' said Cassie, once Julia had gone.

'To satisfy my curiosity.' Charlotte sat down at the table, eyeing her daughter. 'I thought you were giving dinner to someone called Rupert last Friday, not Nick. And,' she added relentlessly, 'you told me the same Rupert was giving you a lift down today. Instead it's Nick again. Am I reading too much into all this?'

'Of course you are,' said Cassie firmly, and gave brief explanations.

Charlotte looked unconvinced, but Nick put an end to her questions by coming in with Alice, a triumphant Emily riding on his shoulders.

'I'll take the dogs out before I have any coffee,' said Bill Lovell.

'Can I come?' asked Alice eagerly.

'Of course. Get your things.'

Julia took a protesting Emily from Nick's shoulders,

diverting her by holding her up to watch Alice frisking outside in the snow with the ecstatic dogs.

'Are you meeting up with someone at this hotel, Nick?' asked Mrs Lovell casually.

'I'm afraid not.'

'Then Bill and I insist you spend Christmas here.'

Cassie's eyes widened in shock, and after a swift look at her face, Nick shook his head.

'That's very kind of you, but I couldn't possibly trespass on your hospitality to that extent—'

'Think of Alice,' advised Mrs Lovell. 'She wouldn't miss Max so much if you were here.'

Julia turned from the window to set Emily on her feet. 'You're right, Mother. It's a brilliant idea. Nick can sleep in the spare room; Alice can go in with Cassie. And there's enough food here for an army.'

Nick shot a searching blue glance at Cassie. 'It's very good of you, Mrs Lovell, but—'

'Will you lose any money on the hotel deal?' asked Cassie practically.

'That's not the point!'

'Then stay.' She relented, smiling at him. 'Don't worry, my mother's a much better cook than I am.'

When Alice returned and heard the news she was euphoric. 'Uncle Nick, are you really going to stay here too?' she demanded, her eyes like stars.

'Apparently so,' he said, hugging her, and looked over the curly head at Cassie. 'We're very lucky, you and I, Alice.'

The child nodded vigorously, then her glow faded a little. 'I wish Daddy would come too.'

'I know, sweetheart. But Daddy will be very pleased to know you're having such a great time with everyone here,' Nick assured her. 'How about you and I go out and do some shopping?' He looked at Cassie. 'Can I persuade you to do your Good Samaritan act again and show us the best places?'

Cassie, who had spent the last few minutes coming to terms with the idea of Nick as an extra guest for Christmas, decided to go with the flow. 'On one condition, she said firmly. 'We walk. I've had enough skidding about in cars for a while. Besides, you'll never park anywhere in town on Christmas Eve.'

'Do you mind?' said Nick quietly, as Alice skipped ahead of them later along Ashdown Lane.

'No,' said Cassie.

He gave her a wry look. 'Just "no".'

'Do you want me to say I'm delighted?'

'Yes.'

'Then I will. I'm delighted you're staying for Christmas, Dominic Seymour. Is that better?'

'Marginally.' He took her hand and pulled her to a halt, looking down into her eyes. 'Say the word and I can still push on to the hotel.'

Cassie's eyes fell. 'It might snow again.'

'Does that mean you want me to stay?'

'Yes.'

Nick bent suddenly and kissed her hard.

'Why are you kissing Cassie?' demanded Alice, running back to them.

Nick caught her up and spun her round. 'Because it's Christmas, sweetheart. Come on, let's go or the shops will shut before we get there!'

Cassie watched them, laughing, and decided her best plan was to put last night from her mind, enjoy Christmas and forget that Nick was anything to do with Max Seymour. Shopping with Nick, as she already knew, was an exhilarating experience. He rushed them in and out of shops like a whirlwind. Sometimes one of them left the other with a giggling Alice to make secret purchases, and at others they consulted with the little girl very seriously on the choice of gifts for Cassie's parents and Julia.

'To show my gratitude to Cassie's family for inviting me for Christmas,' Nick explained to Alice, and she nodded gravely.

'I went shopping with Julia and bought them presents with my pocket money.'

'Good girl.'

They bought vintage port for Bill Lovell, and a cashmere scarf Alice chose in pimento-red for Charlotte. But for Julia, to Cassie's surprise, Nick chose an expensive, but impersonal dried flower arrangement from the florist in the arcade.

'That flat of hers needs cheering up a bit,' he told Cassie, as the flowers were gift-wrapped.

What had she imagined he'd buy Julia—sexy underwear? thought Cassie irritably.

After buying a few last-minute items on the list her mother had given her, they had tea and cakes in a smart tea-shop in the arcade, Alice's face so happy Cassie was reconciled to the thought of Nick Seymour for company over Christmas. In the middle of telling Alice a story about getting stuck in the sand in the desert, he turned to find Cassie watching him, and his eyes lit with a heat which made her heart thump. She looked away quickly, afraid of where all this was leading, and with a wry, crooked smile Nick finished off the tale.

Later that evening, when dinner was over and Alice and Emily in bed, the others were lazing in front of a roaring fire in the small sitting-room. Bill Lovell and

Nick were watching the news on TV, and Charlotte was checking that she'd done everything possible in the way of preparations without actually cooking the Christmas dinner.

'Mother, stop worrying,' said Cassie. 'The turkey's stuffed and waiting in the scullery—hopefully safe from the dogs—the pudding's ready and the mince pies are made. The fridge is loaded. We've eaten that terrible dinner tonight—'

'Terrible?' Nick looked across in amazement.

Julia nodded. 'No first course. And just home-baked ham with scalloped potatoes and so on, and ordinary old apple pie.'

Everyone laughed, and Charlotte Lovell eyed her daughters with dignity. 'You may well tease. But if I'd known Nick was dining with us I'd have achieved something better.'

'I doubt you could have, from my point of view,' he assured her.

'But just think what you might have been eating at the hotel!'

'Ah, but I would have been eating it alone, Mrs Lovell.'

'That's a shameless bid for sympathy,' said Cassie, and everyone laughed. Except Julia.

'Don't upset yourself—he'll turn up, Jules,' she said later in the kitchen, as they were making coffee.

'I don't know why I'm worrying! If Max does turn up he won't want to see me.'

Cassie looked at her sister with compassion. 'You still love him, then.'

'Yes. Unfortunately. One-man woman, that's me. The curse of the Lovells. Dad's always been the only man for Mother, and I'm the same about Max. So choose carefully, Cassie,' warned Julia. 'It's probably in the genes.'

When they rejoined the others Charlotte Lovell looked up hopefully. 'I don't suppose either of you would fancy going to church tonight? One of us should. Bill won't, of course, the heathen. And I'm too tired.'

'I wonder why?' said her husband dryly.

'I can't, sorry,' said Julia. 'I've got Emily.'

Cassie nodded, resigned. 'All right. I'll go.'

'I'll come with you,' said Nick quickly.

She stared at him in surprise. 'Are you sure? You don't have to.'

'I'd like to.'

'All right—half an hour, then. And wrap up, because I'd rather walk than go by car.'

Well aware that her family was taking a keen interest in the situation, Cassie set off with Nick later, both of them wearing boots and muffled in scarves, Cassie's wool beret pulled low over her eyes.

'This is something of a surprise,' she said breathlessly, as they trudged as quickly as possible over the snow-covered ruts in the lane. 'I wouldn't have put you down as a churchgoer, Nick.'

'I'm not. I last went to church when Max married Julia. Watch out,' he warned as Cassie slithered perilously. He took her gloved hand in his. 'And I was obliged to attend chapel in school, of course.'

'So why did you come tonight?'

'To be with you,' he said simply, silencing her so completely there was no more conversation until they reached the main road into town. 'I wanted you to myself, to ask if you mind spending Christmas with the enemy,' he said eventually.

'No.' Which was true. She no longer thought of Nick as the enemy.

Nick turned her to face him under the first streetlight they came to. 'I'll be based in this country for the foreseeable future.'

Cassie gazed up at him warily. 'Are you pleased?'

'Very.'

Nick bent towards her involuntarily, then straightened as they heard voices approaching. He smiled into her eyes. 'This is the most interesting Christmas I've ever spent. And it promises to be one of the most frustrating at the same time.'

'Frustrating?' demanded Cassie, as they resumed their walk towards the sound of church bells.

'I'm very grateful for your family's hospitality, Cassandra Lovell, but it has one big disadvantage. A good guest doesn't shock his hosts by making love to their daughter. Much as he wants to.'

'Even if said daughter were likely to co-operate,' she said tartly. 'And since you've brought the subject up I'd like to make it clear I take full responsibility for what happened at the farm. But it was an accident, a one-off. And for reasons you know as well as I do, Dominic Seymour, it's not going to happen again.'

The service was beautiful, as usual, the old Norman church at its best, with lighted candles flickering on the red cassocks and gleaming young faces of the choirboys, the familiar carols sung with enthusiasm by the large, festive congregation.

'I enjoyed that,' said Nick, as they came out into the freezing night air afterwards.

Thoughts of Nick's previous visit to the church kept

Cassie silent for a while as they trudged through the silent town.

'What's the matter?' he asked at last.

'I was thinking of Julia's wedding.'

'With very little pleasure, obviously.'

'All the joy and wonder of that day, the work my mother did to organise everything to perfection, Julia's happiness—all of it wasted.'

'And you blame me.'

Cassie shook her head, shivering a little, and Nick quickened their pace. 'No. Not now, anyway. After the break-up I was furious with both Seymours. You for being in the wrong place at the wrong time, and Max for being so pathologically jealous he could actually believe Julia had been unfaithful to him.'

When they reached the trees flanking the gateway to the Lovell house Nick halted, and looked down at Cassie in the cold moonlight.

'He's never divorced her, has he?'

'No.'

'And from his address book it's obvious he keeps track of her.'

Cassie shrugged. 'Perhaps he's trying to catch Julia with a lover so he *can* divorce her. Not that he ever will. Julia's a one-man woman. She still loves Max.'

'I'd lay bets he feels the same,' said Nick with conviction. 'Only he's so damned proud and unbending he can't bring himself to make any more overtures.'

'Nor can Julia.'

'Isn't there something we can do about it? If Julia really does love him, perhaps Max should be told.'

'Best not to interfere. You never know—Alice's Christmas with us might break the ice.'

'Let's hope you're right, but before we go in,' added Nick, 'answer one question for me, Cassie.'

'What?' she said warily.

'You made yourself pretty plain where I'm concerned before we went into church. But if I was someone else, neither Seymour nor Max's brother, would you still be so adamant?' Nick's face was a stern study in black and white in the moonlight as his eyes bored down into hers.

Cassie met them without evasion. 'No,' she admitted reluctantly, and Nick caught her in his arms and kissed her very thoroughly.

'Merry Christmas, Cassie,' he whispered, when he raised his head.

She breathed in shakily. 'Merry Christmas, Nick.'

They climbed the steep curves of the drive in oddly companionable silence, trying to tread softly as they made their way round the back of the house.

'I'm tired,' whispered Cassie, 'so let's make sure the dogs don't bark or the girls will think Father Christmas has arrived and demand to open their stockings!'

'Do you think Alice still believes in him?' asked Nick, as they let themselves in by the back door.

'Of course she does, because she wants to,' said Cassie, stooping to make a fuss of the sleepy retrievers.

Nick smiled at her crookedly. 'This year I think I believe in him myself!'

CHAPTER NINE

CHRISTMAS morning began early in the Lovell household. Emily discovered a bulging stocking hanging at the end of her cot and woke her mother in excitement, which roused an equally excited Alice when she spotted the stocking hanging over the fireplace.

'Come on, then,' said Cassie, yawning. 'Let's join Julia and Emily. Dressing-gowns on first.'

After much kissing and Christmas greetings, Cassie got into bed with Julia, with the two little girls between them as they emptied their stockings. Alice helped Emily, their two curly bronze heads close together, and Julia gazed at them with a longing Cassie couldn't bear to witness.

'I might as well go downstairs to let the dogs out, and put the oven on ready for the turkey,' she said, sliding out of bed. 'I'll see you girls later.'

As she tiptoed along the corridor the door to the spare room opened, and Nick stood in the doorway in his dressing-gown, rubbing a hand along his stubble-roughened jaw. 'Merry Christmas again, Cassie,' he whispered.

'Same to you, Nick. Hope we didn't wake you.'

He shook his head, grinning. 'What time do you want me up?'

'Whenever you like. I'm going down to make some tea for Mother and Dad, then I'll be back up to dress.'

After turning the bouncing retrievers out to play in the snow, Cassie switched on the oven, made tea, laid a small tray, let the dogs back in, gave them a filled bowl each, then took the tray up to her parents, insisting they stay there for a while in peace.

'I'll put the turkey in, *and* get breakfast,' she said firmly. 'No bacon and eggs for anyone this morning.'

Her mother frowned. 'But Nick might like some—'

'Tough,' said Cassie. 'He's not getting any.'

Bill Lovell laughed and propped himself up to drink his tea. 'And how are my little darlings this morning?'

'We're all fine,' said Cassie, grinning, and dashed off.

Later, in jeans and scarlet sweater, her hair tied up with a red ribbon, Cassie went down to put the turkey in and lay the breakfast table to an accompaniment of carols from the radio, humming as she put bread in the toaster and poured orange juice into her mother's best crystal jug.

'You sound happy,' said Nick from the doorway.

She looked up with a smile. 'In case you hadn't noticed, it's Christmas. Popular time in our house. Any sign of Julia and the girls?'

'There was a lot of loud protesting from somewhere.'

'Emily getting dressed. Not her favourite thing.'

Eventually the entire household sat down to a lively breakfast, and for once Julia and Cassie forced their mother to sit still while they supplied everyone with cereal, toast and fruit, and poured juice, tea and coffee, according to requirements, letting Alice help Emily with her meal.

Later, after the turkey had been well basted and the vegetables swiftly prepared, everyone went along to the drawing-room to make a start on the miniature mountain of presents piled under the twinkling lights of the tall Christmas tree.

Soon the carpet disappeared under a mass of discarded

wrapping paper, as squeals of delight from Emily greeted puzzles and toys, including Paddington Bear, while Alice glowed with pleasure as she unwrapped books and clothes, and the music centre Nick had bought her, with a supply of compact discs from Cassie.

Some of the gifts were costly, others silly and inexpensive, but all were received in the same spirit. Nick unwrapped a navy cashmere scarf, the twin of the gift he'd purchased for Charlotte, and looked up at Cassie with a wry smile.

'So that's why you were whispering with Alice! Thank you.'

'And here's something from me,' said Julia, handing him a small parcel.

He looked taken aback. 'Julia, there was no need—'

'I had four done. One for Mother and Dad, another for Cassie, and two spares, so I thought you'd like one,' she said matter-of-factly. 'I took the photograph as soon as we arrived and the pharmacy in town did a rush job to print them.'

Nick took off the paper to disclose a photograph of Emily and Alice smiling happily from a small silver frame, the curly chestnut heads close together, Alice's arm protective round the toddler. 'It's lovely, Julia,' he said quietly. 'Thank you.'

'I thought you'd like it.' Julia smiled at him. 'And thank you for the flower arrangement. Exactly to my taste.' She looked under the tree. 'I think that's the lot.'

'Not quite,' said her mother, taking a small package from a branch of the Christmas tree. 'This one seems to be for you, Cassie.'

'You're really spoiling me this year,' said Cassie, who was already in possession of earrings and underwear and a generous cheque.

'It's not from us,' said her father, peering over his wife's shoulder.

Cassie shot a glance at Nick, but he was busy pushing Emily on a brightly-coloured plastic train when she opened the package to discover a wide silver bangle she'd cast covetous eyes at in Harrods. The initial 'C' had been added to the central garland of engraved flowers, and she stared at it, biting her lip.

'Heavens, Cassie,' said Julia. 'That's gorgeous!'

Alice jumped up to see, and the senior Lovells joined in her exclamations as Cassie looked over their heads at Nick.

'Thank you. It's beautiful—but you were much too extravagant.' *And* clever—to get it engraved with her initial so she was bound to accept it.

'Just a small token of appreciation for all your help,' he assured her.

'Right,' said Charlotte Lovell, after a glancc at her daughter's flushed face. 'Time to concentrate on lunch. I need volunteers. Dogs to be walked, dining-room table to be laid and an assistant for sauces, please.'

The men went out into the garden with the dogs and a heavily wrapped Emily, Alice helped Julia with the table, and Cassie enveloped herself in a large apron and under close supervision saw to bread sauce and the gravy for the turkey, but firmly delegated the brandy sauce to Julia. Afterwards everyone went to change into festive clothes for the special meal, the men in suits, Cassie in her burgundy dévoré dress, Charlotte in rose-pink wool, Julia in clinging jersey the colour of her eyes. A protesting Emily had been changed into a green velvet dress with white collar and smocking, and Alice was very pleased with herself in Julia's gift of navy tights and roll-necked sweater with a flowered denim mini-skirt.

'How do I look, Uncle Nick?' she demanded, pirouetting.

'Grown up and gorgeous,' he said promptly.

It was a very festive company who sat down in the dining-room to enjoy turkey with all the trimmings. Alice's face glowed as she sat next to Julia, with Emily on the other side in her highchair, as crackers were pulled, the jokes groaned over, and party hats adjusted to jaunty angles.

Nick looked down at the wide bangle on Cassie's wrist as she took the chair next to him.

'You weren't pleased,' he said in an undertone.

'I hadn't expected anything so extravagant.'

There was no more opportunity for private conversation as they passed dishes and Cassie's father poured wine he'd been keeping for the occasion. Once they'd eaten the main course, Nick got to his feet and raised his glass.

'I'd like to propose a toast,' he said, as expectant faces turned towards him. 'To the entire, hospitable Lovell family, for inviting Alice and me to share in your Christmas.'

There was a concerted murmur of thanks round the table, then Julia raised her own glass. 'To absent friends.'

The others echoed the toast, and Cassie jumped up quickly to clear plates before emotion could spoil the occasion. When the pudding was brought in Julia circled with her camera, taking pictures of Emily and Alice as her father poured brandy over the pudding and set it alight. When Emily clapped her hands in glee Alice kissed her chubby cheek impulsively.

'Isn't she cute?' she said to Cassie.

'Very. So are you, darling!'

It was late afternoon by the time the meal was over and cleared away. Julia took an unwilling Emily off for a nap, informing the company that she might well lie on her bed herself, to encourage her daughter to sleep. Alice went for a walk with Mr Lovell, and Nick and the dogs, and Cassie sent her mother off to her room for a rest.

'Go on,' she said imperiously. 'Dad can have a snooze in the study when he comes in, and the rest of us can loll about by the fire and gradually recover. Great meal, Mother.'

Charlotte Lovell kissed her daughter and tapped the wrist adorned with the silver bangle. 'Nice,' she said, eyes twinkling, and took herself off.

'What happens now?' said Nick, when he brought Alice back to join Cassie.

'We play games, or sleep, or talk, or just do nothing,' said Cassie, yawning. 'Take your pick. You could put a log or two on the fire first.'

They played Scrabble with Alice as the sky darkened outside, and eventually Julia returned with Emily, who had vociferously refused to stay away from the fun.

Once she was reunited with Alice the little girl was happy to play with her toys, showing remarkable skill with the new wooden jigsaw puzzles she'd been given.

'How about some tea?' said Julia after a while, and waved Cassie back to her seat. 'No. You stay there, love. You've done quite enough for one day. I'll see to this.'

Nick and Cassie sat together in companionable silence on a sofa, watching the two curly heads bent together over the puzzles.

'All this is very different from the way I expected to spend Christmas,' he said quietly. 'I hope my presence didn't spoil things for you. I had my doubts when I saw your reaction to the bracelet.'

'Sorry I was ungracious,' she murmured. 'But I know exactly what it cost, remember.' She smiled at him wryly, then frowned. 'Did you hear something?'

'Yes, I did.' He got up quickly and went over to a window. 'Are you expecting visitors?'

Cassie shook her head. 'People come in for drinks on Boxing Day, but today is strictly a family day—though you're right. That's the doorbell. Dad will answer it. Probably someone for him or Mother.'

But at the sound of voices Alice looked up in sudden hope, joy dawning in her eyes as deep, unmistakable tones mingled with Bill Lovell's. *'Daddy!'* she cried, and shot to her feet to run from the room.

'Hell, she's right.' Nick yanked Cassie to her feet. 'Come here!'

Emily looked up at them, round-eyed, as Nick rushed Cassie towards the mistletoe hanging from one of the overhead lights and smothered her protest with a kiss better suited to the bedroom than under the mistletoe. He held her in an iron grip and went on kissing her until Cassie's head was reeling. When he finally released her she blushed to the roots of her hair as she saw the tall, haggard man eyeing them in astonishment from the doorway, with a euphoric, giggling Alice clinging to his hand.

'The bad penny himself,' said Nick flippantly, out of breath. 'Hello, Max. What took you so long?' He strode forward with outstretched hand, and after a moment's hesitation Max Seymour shook it.

'I was ill and got lost. It's a long story,' he said wearily, his eyes drawn like a magnet to the child playing with her toys.

'Hello,' said Emily, beaming at him. 'I got Paddington.'

'I'll go upstairs and get my wife,' said Bill Lovell, hovering in the doorway. He rolled his eyes at his daughter and went off in a hurry.

Cassie pulled herself together. 'You'd better sit down, Max. Where have you come from?'

'London.' Max Seymour tore his eyes from the toddler with obvious difficulty. 'Thank you, Cassie. I got in from Australia yesterday. Nick left a message to say Alice was here, so I drove up this morning.'

Max Seymour looked ill and strained, with far more grey in the bronze hair than Cassie remembered. He sat with an arm round Alice, his eyes riveted to the small girl playing on the floor.

'That's Emily, Daddy,' said Alice happily. 'Isn't she sweet?'

Emily got up and came to stand in front of them, peering up at Max. 'Got headache?' she asked. 'Want cuppa tea?'

'Emily's cure for all ills,' said Cassie huskily as Max, plainly choked with emotion, touched a hand to the bronze curls. Then he tensed and sprang to his feet as Julia backed in with a loaded tray. She stopped dead at the sight of him, turned white as a sheet and dropped the tray with a crash.

Pandemonium reigned as Cassie snatched Emily up and out of harm's way and Nick leapt to gather up shattered china while Alice ran to comfort Julia and Max Seymour stood staring at his wife like a man turned to stone.

'What on earth's going on?' Charlotte Lovell hurried into the room and took the situation in at a glance. 'Ah. Bill said you'd turned up, Max. Better late than never. Sit down, Julia, before you fall down. Bill, go and get a cloth. Mind you don't cut your fingers, Nick. If you give the baby to Julia, Cassie, you can give me a hand.'

Within minutes the tea was mopped, broken china collected and a second tea-tray provided. And in all the commotion neither Julia nor Max had said a word.

'You look ghastly, Max,' said Charlotte, forthright as usual as she handed him a cup of tea.

'I've been ill,' he said huskily. 'A fever of some kind I picked up in the jungle. I was off my head for a while.'

For the past two years in fact, thought Cassie nastily, eyeing her sister's paper-white face.

'Couldn't you have got in touch in some way?' demanded Nick curtly. 'Alice was worried to death. Hard to believe, but so was I.'

'When I finally made it to civilisation I rang your flat, but with no luck. I couldn't remember which hotel you were going to, and there was no answer from my own place. I spent the entire flight to Heathrow worrying about Alice.' Max Seymour hugged his daughter as she ran back to him. 'When I got to Chiswick I found your message and tried to ring here, but the line must be down. Once I knew Alice was safe, I realised the weather was too bad for driving last night anyway, so I started out this morning instead. The roads are still dicey, which is why I'm so late.'

'Have you eaten?' demanded his practical mother-in-law, making an obvious effort to suppress her hostility.

Max shook his head. 'No, Charlotte. But please don't go to any trouble. I'll take myself off to the King's Head—'

'On Christmas Day?' she said, shaking her head. 'It's been booked solid for months. Just give me a few minutes and I'll rustle something up. Alice, Julia, you can come and help me.'

Julia rose like an automaton, scooped up Emily and, without a word to Max, or a look in his direction, took Alice by the hand and accompanied her mother from the room.

'I'll just see to the dogs,' said Bill Lovell, with a cool, appraising look at his daughter's husband. 'Put some more logs on the fire, Nick.'

Nick obeyed, then resumed his place beside Cassie and put a possessive arm round her. She leaned against him co-operatively, conscious of the haggard man surveying them rather blankly.

'So, Max, are you going to take Alice away now?' she asked bluntly.

Max gave her a twisted smile. 'Straight in with guns blazing, Cassie?'

'Everyone wants to know,' snapped Nick. 'Cassie put it into words first, that's all.'

'No need to jump to her defence,' said Max wryly. 'Do I take it you two are friends these days?'

Nick looked down at Cassie with a smile his brother couldn't fail to interpret. 'More than just friends, Max,' he said. 'Once I talk her out of her animosity towards the Seymour family I'm going to marry her.'

Cassie tensed, but Nick's arm squeezed her waist in warning. She brushed back a lock of hair, and looked Max Seymour in the eye. 'I'm afraid he's got a lot of persuading to do after the way you treated Julia.'

Max winced. 'I've asked Julia to come back to me several times—'

'Do you blame her for refusing?' she snapped, eyes flashing.

'How the hell did you expect her to say yes when you won't let her see Alice?' said Nick angrily. 'And, since we're actually talking face to face about Julia at last, you may like to know she's never so much as let me hold her hand.'

'I know,' said Max hopelessly.

'Has this fever of yours affected your vision,' added Cassie relentlessly, 'or did you take a good look at Emily just now? She's your child, Max.'

'I know that, too.' He gave a sudden groan, like a man in agony, and dropped his head in his hands. 'What in God's name am I going to do? Julia wouldn't even look at me just now. She's never touched a penny of the money I pay into her account every month. I thought keeping her away from Alice would force her hand, make her come back to me—'

'Have you tried a simple apology?' said Nick dryly. 'Better still, just tell her you love her, you idiot.'

Max's head went up, his eyes blazing with outrage for a moment, and Cassie stiffened. But Nick held her closer, his eyes fixed on his brother's face in challenge, and Max deflated suddenly, looking tired and utterly despondent.

'It's obviously too late for that. Julia can't forgive me. Why should she? I can't forgive myself. She's so beautiful I've always been jealous of every man who even looked at her.' His eyes met Nick's. 'And don't tell me you weren't in love with her once.'

'I had a crush on her in the beginning, yes,' agreed Nick, his gaze unwavering as it met his brother's bloodshot, weary green eyes. 'But it soon died when I found Julia never had eyes for anyone but you. The day you found us together I was merely comforting her. She wouldn't tell me what was really troubling her, just said she was miserable because you were about to take off for months to the back of beyond somewhere.'

Max said nothing, looking worse than ever.

'So you threw Nick out of the house and refused to believe the child was yours when Julia told you she was pregnant,' went on Cassie, like Nemesis.

Max winced. 'There's more to it than that. I lost my temper and said things I didn't mean, especially about Nick.'

'Damn right,' snapped Nick with hostility, and Cassie put a restraining hand on his arm. 'The first time I saw Julia afterwards was the other night. When I went round to her place to accuse her of making off with Alice,' he added bitterly. 'We Seymours really know how to sweet-talk a woman!'

'Anyway, none of that matters because now you've seen Emily with your own eyes, Max,' said Cassie bluntly. 'You know exactly who her father is.'

'I always have known,' said Max very quietly. 'She's so lovely, Cassie—just like Alice at the same age. Not that Julia is going to let me near her.'

On the point of telling Max how worried Julia had been when he was missing, Cassie changed her mind. He could stew a bit longer. It was up to Julia to tell him that, or not, as she chose.

Charlotte came in with a tray and put it on a table beside Max. 'Just leftovers, I'm afraid. Turkey, of course, and some ham and a spot of salad.'

Max looked at her in appeal. 'Charlotte, I really can't eat anything until I've talked to Julia. Will you ask her to see me? Just for a few minutes. After that, if she wants, I promise I'll leave her in peace.'

'If I ask she'll say no,' said Mrs Lovell, thinking it over. She shrugged. 'Look, Max, go up to the main bathroom. Alice is helping Julia give Emily a bath. Just barge in. With luck, Julia won't throw you out in front of the children.'

When Max had gone, Charlotte picked up the tray again. 'I'll take this back to the kitchen.' She sighed, eyeing Cassie and Nick. 'Would you two mind if I fall apart for a bit with Bill in the other room? All this drama is exhausting. Let me know if there's bloodshed.'

Nick got up and took the tray from her. 'I'll take it, Charlotte. You go off and put your feet up.'

'Thank you. When you see Alice tell her the film she's looking forward to is on in half an hour.'

'Right.'

Left alone for once, Cassie sat staring into the fire, twisting the heavy silver bangle on her wrist as she wondered what was going on upstairs.

'You went a bit far,' she said accusingly, the moment Nick reappeared. 'The kiss was a good idea—'

'A positive brainwave—highly satisfactory in all ways,' he agreed, sitting down beside her.

'Oh, I knew exactly what you were doing,' she assured him. 'But the marrying part was a bit over the top.'

'Max seemed impressed,' he said lightly. 'Which was the object of the exercise. One of them, anyway.'

Cassie heaved a worried sigh. 'What do you suppose is going on up there?'

'No idea. Nor am I going up to find out either! Don't worry, Cassie. Whatever happens, things will be better from now on.'

'Who for?' she demanded.

'Alice, for starters.'

Right on cue, Alice came bouncing into the room, her face one big smile. 'Daddy's helping Julia bath Emily, so I've come down to watch television. Daddy said you're going to marry Uncle Nick, Cassie!'

Cassie stared speechlessly. 'Well, I'm— I mean—'

'It's all a bit new to her yet,' put in Nick quickly. He jumped up and gave his niece a hug. 'Charlotte says your programme's on soon.'

Alice gave him a very grown-up look of understanding. 'You mean you want me to leave you alone so you can kiss Cassie again. All right, I'm going!' She gave them a cheeky wink, and dashed from the room, laughing.

'She'll tell my parents now,' said Cassie, resigned.

'Should I have asked your father first?' enquired Nick.

'No, you should have consulted *me*—'

'Right. Will you marry me, Cassie?' he said promptly.

She glared at him. 'It's not funny!'

Nick sat down and took her hand. 'Look, Cassie, just for now play along. Until Max and Julia sort themselves out, at least. If he thinks I lied he might start wondering why and get suspicious again. It's possible. The workings of Max's mind have always been a mystery to me.'

Cassie eyed him suspiciously, then sighed. 'I suppose so.'

He put a finger under her chin. 'In the meantime, would you be surprised to know Alice was right? I do want to kiss you. Most of the time.' His lips settled on hers by way of illustration. When she made no protest he slid his hands into her hair and held her fast, kissing her with an unexpected tenderness which breached her defences far more than any masterful display of passion.

'Ahem!' said a voice from the doorway, and they sprang apart to see Julia, carrying a dressing-gowned Emily, with Max following behind. He looked less haggard, but totally dazed, as though he found it hard to believe what was happening.

'I'm going to give Max his meal in the kitchen,' announced Julia with composure, eyeing them. 'Can you two be trusted to stop canoodling and entertain Emily for a while—or shall I call Mother?'

'No,' said Cassie and Nick in unison, jumping up.

'Did Max get it wrong?' said Julia, as Cassie took her shining, pink-faced niece in her arms. 'He said you two were talking about marrying. You didn't tell me!'

'It's all happened a bit fast. Blame it on the mistletoe,' said Nick, putting an arm round Cassie. 'Aren't you pleased for us, Julia?'

'Of course I am,' she said sincerely, and gave Max a look. 'Though I must say I'm surprised Cassie's willing to take on a Seymour.'

'So am I,' said Max, meeting the look head-on. 'But Nick and I are only stepbrothers, remember. He's got a lot of his mother in him, so Cassie won't go far wrong.'

Cassie hid her embarrassed face against Emily's curls. 'In the meantime, shall I give this young lady her milk?'

Julia nodded. 'I'll pop it in when it's warm enough.' She went from the room, drawing Max along with a glance, and Cassie let out the breath she'd been holding as the door closed.

'Do drawing,' said Emily imperiously, struggling to get down.

'Right.' Cassie put her down on the floor, found the new box of crayons and some sheets of stiff paper, and gave a challenging look at Nick. 'How good are you at this kind of thing?'

'More draftsman than artist. But anything to oblige a lady. Especially one as irresistible as this one.'

'Draw teddy,' demanded Emily, then, at a look from Cassie, added, 'Please?' in tones which rendered her uncle helpless.

'You're a charmer,' he informed her.

'It's her Lovell genes,' said Cassie sweetly. 'Certainly not her father's.'

'He must have something to recommend him,' said Nick as he began to draw. 'Otherwise why would Julia still care for him?'

'You've got a point,' conceded Cassie grudgingly. 'I suppose it's always a mystery why a man and woman are attracted to each other.'

'Not in my case,' said Nick softly, looking up at her. 'I know exactly why I'm attracted to you, Cassie Lovell.'

'So do I,' she snapped. 'It's my novelty value in one specific area!'

The blue eyes glittered dangerously. 'Is it so hard to believe I'd like us to spend time together? Not Cassie, Julia's sister, or Nick, Max's brother. Just you and me. Two people with their own identities.' He looked down as a small hand tugged at his sleeve. 'My apologies, Miss Seymour—back to the drawing board.'

CHAPTER TEN

NICK took himself off early on Boxing Day, despite the Lovells' assurances that he was welcome to stay. One Seymour at a time, he told Charlotte with a smile, was quite enough. He expressed his gratitude for their hospitality, said goodbye to everyone, then asked Cassie to walk down to the car to see him off.

'Where are you going?' she asked casually. 'On to the hotel as planned?'

'No. Back to London.'

In which case, thought Cassie irritably, he might have waited and driven her back next day. 'You're welcome to stay.'

Nick leaned against the bonnet of the car. 'The thaw is well underway, so driving back's no problem. Now Max is here it's best I make myself scarce, leave Julia to work things out with him free of my presence. Besides, since you insisted on letting your family in on our little charade, I find it hard to act naturally when Max is around.'

'Doesn't he think it strange that you're leaving?'

'I told him I had to tear myself away from you to write a report before I get back to work.' Nick smiled wryly. 'And, to be honest, sharing a room with Max is quite a strain.'

'Why?'

'It's not only the first time in our lives, but I'm certain he didn't sleep a wink last night. Probably because he wanted to share Julia's room, not mine.'

'He surely didn't expect her to welcome him straight into her bed with open arms!' said Cassie scornfully.

'I don't suppose he did. But it didn't stop him wanting that. And in a way it's a pity it wasn't possible,' added Nick frankly. 'Sharing a bed can solve a lot of problems.'

She glared at him. 'If you mean—'

'I *meant*,' he said mockingly, 'that for you and me, Cassandra Lovell, it was a wonderful way to keep warm.'

'Thanks a lot!'

Nick shook his head at her reprovingly and took her in his arms. 'Max is watching,' he whispered, and kissed her at length before he let her go. 'I'll ring when you get back to London.'

Cassie watched the car disappear down the bends of the drive, then went back into the house, feeling utterly flat and in no mood for the ritual Boxing Day lunchtime drinks party.

'Where's Max?' she asked, as she joined the others in the kitchen.

'In the bath,' said her sister, surprised. 'Why?'

'No reason.' So he hadn't been watching. Cassie's spirits rose. 'Right. What can I do to help?'

When Cassie's train got in next day she was enveloped in an embrace the moment she put a foot on the platform.

'Rupert!' she said, struggling to look pleased. 'How did you know which train I was catching?'

'Your friend Jane gave me your parents' telephone number,' he said, smiling, looking elegantly countrified in a brand new canvas poacher's jacket. He picked up her bag. 'I thought I'd give you a lift.'

'How very nice of you.' Cassie pulled herself together, doing her best to sound grateful. 'I hoped someone would meet me.' Someone else. Nick Seymour, for instance.

The journey to Shepherd's Bush was enlivened by Rupert's account of Christmas with his family and the parties he'd been to. 'How about you, Cassie?' he asked eventually. 'What sort of Christmas did you have?'

'Lovely, but exhausting.'

When they got to the house Rupert seemed to take it for granted Cassie would invite him in, and since he'd taken the trouble to meet her train she introduced him to Polly and gave him coffee, but after half an hour or so sent him firmly on his way.

'I'd hoped to take you out tonight, Cassie,' he said on the doorstep, obviously reluctant to leave. 'Won't you change your mind?'

'Could we postpone it to another time soon? Monday?' She smiled at him brightly. 'I need a breather to recover from Christmas.'

Cassie's real reason for staying in was to wait for a call from Nick. She rang her mother to report in, and heard diplomatic relations between Julia and Max were still improving. Later she washed her hair, shared supper with Polly, exchanged news of the holidays, did some planning for the party on New Year's Eve, and finished some ironing she'd had no time for before she went home for Christmas. At last she gave up waiting for Nick to ring, and went to bed.

Next day, sorry now she'd left Chastlecombe so soon, Cassie helped her friends with the housework, then went out with Polly for a snack lunch and some necessary food shopping. When they arrived back there was a scribbled note from Jane.

Gone out with Giles. Two messages, Cass. One from your sister, one from Nick Seymour. Ring both as soon as you can.

Julia answered the phone almost immediately.

'Cassie? Thank goodness. Max is helping Alice with Emily's bathtime, so listen; I've only got a minute or two. Max needs to be in London on Monday to see his agent, so he wants the three of us to go up with him. And he's so keen to start mending fences with Nick he wants you both round to Chiswick in the evening for a meal to celebrate.'

'Celebrate what, exactly? Are you two back together officially?'

'We've agreed to try again, yes. But on my terms.'

'Which are?'

'We take things slowly. Get to know each other all over again.'

'Is he happy with that?'

'Not the slow bit. But at the moment Max is ready to do whatever I want. I'm afraid the celebrating part is about you two. After seeing you together, Max begged my forgiveness for his jealousy of Nick, practically on bended knees. And, take note, Cassie, he thinks you and Nick have been together for quite a while, not just five minutes.'

'Oh, wonderful—now Nick and I have to make like lovebirds whenever Max is around, I suppose!'

'Yes, please. But it's not for long. He takes up the post in Cambridge at the beginning of term. You can busk it until then, surely?'

'I suppose so.' Cassie hesitated. 'Julia, are you going with him?'

'Of course I am. Not that I'm telling him just yet.'

Julia gave a breathless little laugh. 'It's rather fun, dangling him on a string. Especially as Max promises I can see Alice as much as I like in future, whatever I decide.'

Cassie put the phone down and stood staring into space, wrestling with the problem of how to hide her feelings from Nick and pretend to be in love with him at the same time. When the phone rang beside her she snatched it up.

'Cassie? I've been trying to ring you for the past ten minutes,' said Nick impatiently.

'I've been talking to Julia.'

'I thought it might have been young Ashcroft.'

'It might have been,' she agreed, 'but it wasn't. Julia was bringing me up to date on the ceasefire with Max.'

'So you know we're bidden to dine in Chiswick?'

'Yes. Absolutely spiffing. I can't wait,' said Cassie bitterly.

'Look, if you feel like that about it I'll just tell him the truth.'

'No! Don't do that, for heaven's sake. Not now Max is fool enough to believe you've switched your allegiance from Julia to me.'

'Who the devil's been rattling your cage, Cassie?' he demanded. 'Bad day?'

'No worse than usual.'

'So what's the matter?'

She was mad as fire because he hadn't rung the night before, but she wasn't telling him that. 'I'm tired, that's all.'

'Out late last night?' he asked silkily.

Cassie frowned. 'No. I washed my hair and went to bed early.'

There was a lengthy pause. 'Look, Cassie,' said Nick at last, 'are you doing anything tonight?'

'Why?' she said warily.

'Before we play our little comedy tomorrow it might be as well to rehearse our lines a bit. I'll be round in half an hour—'

'No, you won't,' she snapped. 'I have things to do. Come round about nine. If you must.'

'Given such a pressing invitation, how can I refuse?' he said with sarcasm. 'All right. Nine. Can we talk in private? Otherwise we'd better go out.'

'I'll see what I can arrange.'

Cassie had lied. She had nothing to do other than take a bath. Afterwards she scrubbed her face clean, bundled her hair up in an untidy knot, dressed in faded jeans and an elderly pink sweater, added socks and espadrilles, then heated some soup and ate it with a cheese sandwich in the kitchen. When Nick arrived, dead on time, she greeted him with cool formality. He took in her appearance with amusement, slung his jacket on a peg in the hall and followed her into the sitting room.

'Where is everyone?' he asked as she curled up in her usual chair.

'Out.'

In direct contrast to Cassie, Nick looked good, as usual, in black moleskin jeans and a sweater which matched his eyes.

'I'm sorry for getting you into this,' he said abruptly.

She shrugged indifferently. 'It's not for long. Max is taking off for Cambridge soon.'

'Is Julia going with him?'

'Yes. But don't let on you know. She wants Max to fry for a bit.'

'Good for Julia.'

'*I* think he's lucky she'll give him the time of day.'

'He agrees with you.'

'Really? How do you know?' said Cassie, intrigued.

'When Max couldn't get to sleep the night we shared a room he actually talked to me for a while. He was seriously ill in the jungle, apparently, didn't expect to make it. His brush with mortality has really brought him up short, taught him where his priorities lie.'

'So you needn't have bothered with all that nonsense under the mistletoe!'

Nick shrugged. 'If it scotched any last doubts on Max's part it was worth it, surely?'

'I suppose so,' said Cassie grudgingly. 'Want some coffee?'

'No, I don't.' His eyes gleamed coldly. 'What I *want* is to know how Ashcroft knew when you were arriving yesterday.'

Cassie stared at him in surprise. 'How did you know Rupert met me?'

'I came to the station on the same errand. Unfortunately I got snarled up in traffic and arrived just in time to witness the enthusiastic embrace. So I went back the way I came before you noticed me.' His mouth tightened. 'Ludicrous, isn't it?'

Not to Cassie. His statement made her feel a lot better. 'Jane gave him the Chastlecombe number and he rang to find out—' She bit her lip.

'What is it?' he demanded.

'I've just remembered. I'm having dinner with Rupert on Monday night.'

Nick smiled evilly. 'Tell him I've got a prior claim.' He got up, his eyes glittering as they moved over her. 'It's not a damn bit of use, you know, Cassie.'

She looked up at him, eyes narrowed. 'What isn't?'

'Trying to turn me off.' He pulled her to her feet and thrust his hands through her hair, bringing it tumbling round her shoulders. 'Is all this supposed to discourage me?'

Cassie glared at him. 'I always dress like this if I'm not going out.'

'If you say so.' Nick laughed indulgently and pulled her close, tipping her flushed face up to his. 'This is really what I came for—'

'You've got a nerve!' she said hotly, trying to break free.

Nick held her fast, chuckling. 'I *meant* that we need to rehearse before our performance on Monday night.'

'No, we don't,' she retorted. 'All we need to do is hold hands a bit. Max won't expect you to make love to me before his very eyes.'

Without warning Nick picked her up and sat down on the sofa with her, tightening his grip when she tried to scramble away.

'To hell with Max—and any nonsense about rehearsing,' he said roughly. 'I just want to make love to you right now, Cassie. I want to take you to bed, feel your mouth part under mine and your body tremble, hear you plead with me again.'

Cassie let out a smothered sound of rage, so incensed she'd have blacked one of his blue eyes if he'd freed her hands. 'How *could* you throw that in my face?' she said, her voice shaking with fury. 'Let me go!'

Nick did so with such alacrity she fell on her hands and knees in her hurry to get away, then shook him off violently when he sprang to help her up.

'Don't touch me!' Mortified, she scrambled to her feet and hugged her arms across her chest, her dark eyes spitting fire at him. 'Look, Dominic Seymour—'

'So we're back to that again,' he interrupted hotly. 'All right, Cassandra Lovell. I get the message.

Christmas was just a ceasefire, and now it's back to hostilities again. You obviously regret sleeping with the enemy. Because no matter what I say—or do—that's how you think of me.'

'Do you blame me?' she retorted, summoning up ammunition in her defence. 'I've had time to think since I saw you last. To remember what happened when I first came to live here!'

Nick stiffened. 'What do you mean?'

'You know exactly what I mean. When you got back from Nigeria, you made some frantic phone calls here, trying to trace Julia. Lucky for you I never answered when you rang, but she'd given strict instructions to the others anyway, so you never found out where she was.'

'Of course I was frantic!' he said bitterly. 'It was only then I discovered what had happened. Max was off in some wilderness, Alice packed off to boarding school, and Julia nowhere to be found. Your parents wouldn't tell me a thing.'

'And you were obviously desperate to find her.'

'Is that so astonishing?' he demanded. 'I wanted to apologise, make amends somehow—'

'And step straight into Max's place in Julia's bed, of course.'

Nick's head went back as though she'd hit him. For a moment there was such menace in the dark-fringed eyes Cassie backed away in alarm.

'Don't worry, I won't touch you.' His voice was vibrant with distaste, and something else Cassie couldn't quite classify. 'All right. You win. Nothing I say is going to change your obstinate little mind about me, so I'll take myself off before I do something I'll regret.'

Cassie had already done something she regretted. She would have given anything to take her last accusation back. She didn't even believe it any more. She'd just needed Nick to tell her *she* was the one he was in love with, not Julia. That making love together at the farm had been a whole lot more than mere propinquity—and sex. But even as she was trying desperately to find the words to tell Nick this he gave up waiting for her to speak and strode out into the hall. He collected his jacket and turned at the front door as she followed him out.

'I'll call for you at eight on Monday,' he said, looming tall and hostile in the narrow space.

She stared at him blankly. 'But that's not— I mean, I don't want—'

'Just for once,' he interrupted harshly, 'forget what *you* want or don't want, Cassie. This is for Julia, and Alice and Emily. One evening out of your life. So cancel Ashcroft and be ready at eight sharp.' He opened the door and went out, slamming it behind him in a way which put the finishing touch to Cassie's evening.

She turned back along the narrow hall in misery, then rang Rupert to leave a message, saying a family crisis made it impossible for her to see him on Monday night after all, and softened the blow by saying she was looking forward to welcoming him to the party on New Year's Eve.

'See you on Monday at the bank, Rupert,' she added, and rang off.

Sunday was a long, difficult day, trying to convince Jane and Polly that nothing was wrong. Cassie gave serious thought to coming down with a bout of fictitious flu to avoid the dinner party, but Julia put paid to that idea by bringing Alice and Emily round in the afternoon, soon after Max had driven them to Chiswick.

While Polly and Jane entertained the children in the sitting-room Julia followed her sister to the kitchen.

'Why aren't you slaving over a hot stove in Chiswick, preparing delicacies for tomorrow night?' said Cassie, filling the coffee machine.

'Mother gave me some cheese soufflés from the freezer to bring with me,' said Julia. 'They're ready to rise up again in splendour tomorrow for the first course, and lovely Janet's doing the rest. But I haven't come here to discuss menus.'

'I didn't think you had,' muttered Cassie, putting mugs on a tray. 'How are things with Max?'

'Going much better than I ever dreamed. He's besotted with Emily, and she with him. And Alice, of course, is floating around on a pink cloud.' Julia fixed her sister with a look of steel. 'I don't want anything to change that. For either of them.'

'Neither do I.'

'Good. Because Max, and I quote, is ''utterly delighted'' to see you so much in love with Nick.'

Cassie sighed. 'All right, I hear you. I'll play nice tomorrow, I promise.'

'But nothing over the top,' warned Julia. 'Max is no fool.'

'I disagree with you there,' said Cassie bitingly, then bit her lip. 'Sorry, Jules. When are you off to Cambridge?'

'Why?'

'It would be a relief to see you settled and happy at last. Alice, too. Have you told Max you're going with him?'

'No. I thought I'd leave that until tonight. Now we're on our own.' Julia flushed.

Cassie looked away, embarrassed. 'I suppose that means you're ready to kiss and make up.'

Julia cleared her throat. 'Living together as friends hasn't been easy.'

'You mean Max is getting impatient?'

'I am, too,' said Julia honestly. 'It's been a long time, and I still love him to bits, no matter what he's done.' She paused. 'Look, Cassie, there's something you ought to know. It might help you to understand why Max behaved like he did.'

'There's no excuse for the way he behaved,' said Cassie scornfully.

'Possibly not. But there is a reason.'

Cassie stared at her sister in sudden consternation. 'You mean he had cause to be jealous of Nick?'

'Certainly not,' said Julia heatedly. 'Once you get an idea into your head it's certainly hard to shift, Cassandra Lovell. And,' she added, 'pretty insulting to me, too.'

'Sorry! So what's this reason, then?'

'Max's first wife, Celia.' Julia drank down some coffee. 'She had a heart defect Max didn't know about. When Alice was born she had an emergency Caesarean section, and her heart didn't stand up to it.'

'I didn't know all the details,' said Cassie quietly. 'Poor Celia.'

'So when we got married Max flatly refused to let me get pregnant, afraid the same thing would happen to me. Birth control was always his responsibility, but for once his method failed.'

'So that's why Max wouldn't believe he was the father!'

'He went berserk with fear when I gave him the glad news, in such a state he hurled the most hurtful thing he could think of at me. The one thing I couldn't take. Nick had enjoyed flirting with me in the past—harmlessly, I may add. But I've never loved anyone but Max from the first day I met him.'

'So he still feels jealous of Nick, then?'

'No. Not now he's seen you together. But I made it clear I needed a demonstration of total trust. No more jealousy, or it's over for good this time.'

In other words, thought Cassie afterwards, if her act with Nick was unconvincing, Max need only look doubtful for a second to make Julia shy away and they'd all be back to square one.

Cassie got home late from a busy day at the bank next day, with no enthusiasm at all for the evening ahead. Nevertheless she took great care with her appearance as she got ready, trying to ignore the nerves which clutched at her like grappling irons. She left her hair loose, and instead of a dress wore black velvet jeans and her newish bronze velvet shirt with the burnt-out fleur-de-lys pattern. To boost her morale, Cassie used every cosmetic aid she possessed, plus a couple of Polly's for luck, added the silver earrings her parents had given her, and after a moment's hesitation slid the wide silver bangle on her wrist. She wasn't sure if Max knew Nick had given it to her, but it was possible. And no stone must be left unturned to convince Max Seymour she was madly in love with his brother. Which shouldn't really be all that difficult. It was the simple truth. Not that anything connected with the Seymours was ever simple.

But when Nick arrived Cassie's resolution almost failed her, He was impressive in a dark city suit and a shirt which matched blue eyes like orbs of black-fringed ice.

'Good evening,' he said with daunting formality as she let him in. 'Are you ready?'

'Yes,' she returned, equally cool. 'I'll just get my coat.'

Nick held her black mohair jacket punctiliously, and Cassie shrugged into it, then dodged away quickly, wishing now she was going out with Rupert, as originally planned. She knew now that Rupert would never be more than a casual friend, but his company would have been infinitely preferable to someone who obviously regretted he'd ever laid eyes on her.

'We've a few minutes yet,' said Nick curtly, 'so let's make a few rules.'

'Rules?'

'For starters, don't shrink away from me like that.'

She glared at him, eyes flashing. 'It's hard not to, in the circumstances.'

'What circumstances?' he demanded.

'Knowing you'd rather be somewhere else, as far away from me as you can get!'

Nick shrugged. 'You made me angry last time we met, Cassie.'

'You still are.'

'Not at all. What man could remain angry with such a ravishing companion for the evening?' he said suavely.

Cassie made for the door before she gave way to impulse and hit him. 'Let's go then, *darling*.'

They completed the journey in frigid silence, but when Nick parked near the Chiswick house he put a hand on her arm as she undid her seat belt.

'Before we go in I'd better provide the final, irrefutable touch of proof.' Nick reached for her left hand, pulled off her glove, then rammed a ring home on her third finger.

'What *are* you doing?' she demanded angrily, rubbing her throbbing knuckle.

'Giving you a ring.'

'I'd gathered that,' she said with sarcasm. 'Whose is it?'

'Yours, for tonight. Try not to lose it.'

Small chance of that, thought Cassie resentfully. It felt like a manacle. But as the security lights flashed on outside the house when they reached the door she peered in dismay at the wide gold band set with three oblong baguette diamonds.

'Nick—' she began, but the door opened and Max stood there, smiling at them in welcome, and Julia came running down the stairs with Alice to greet them, both of them radiant, Julia in her violet cashmere dress and Alice in her much loved mini-skirt.

'Come in, come in,' said Max, looking very different from the haggard man who'd gatecrashed the Lovell Christmas. He smiled ruefully at Cassie. 'Am I allowed a kiss?'

Cassie, aware he was asking for more than that, raised her face. A kiss he could have. Forgiveness took longer. Max smiled wryly in comprehension, kissed her on both cheeks, then let Julia and Alice take her upstairs to take off her coat while he gave his brother a drink.

Nick looked up at Cassie as she went upstairs. 'Don't be long, darling.'

She gave him a smouldering smile, and pushed back a strand of hair. 'I won't.'

'As I said yesterday,' hissed Julia, as Alice ran off to check on Emily, 'don't overdo it.'

'I thought that was pretty good, myself,' said Cassie, injured.

But Julia was staring at the ring. 'Dear me, where did that come from?'

'Nick produced it five minutes ago.' Cassie eyed it

askance. 'It looks horribly valuable. Luckily it's a bit tight. Otherwise I'd be in a state, afraid to lose the thing.'

'If that doesn't convince Max nothing will,' said Julia, impressed.

Cassie looked at her anxiously. 'Look, Jules, is this charade absolutely vital? I can't help feeling worried.'

Julia seemed unconcerned. 'Don't be. This is the icing on the cake, that's all.' She looked up with a smile as Alice came in. 'Is Emily asleep, darling?'

'She'd kicked her covers off, so I tucked her up,' said Alice, pleased with herself. 'Emily's sharing my bedroom, Cassie. I'll go up to bed and read soon, so Julia won't worry about her. Wow, I like that!' she added, eyeing Cassie's shirt. 'You look gorgeous.'

Downstairs, on the sofa where he'd once comforted Julia with such far-reaching results, Nick took Cassie's hand in his, and sat so close she could hardly breathe.

'Alice can have a sip of champagne before she goes up,' said Max, to his daughter's delight, and handed Cassie a glass, then stared, arrested, at her left hand.

'So you've parted with Eileen's ring at last, Nick,' he said quietly.

CHAPTER ELEVEN

HIS *mother's* ring? Colour flooded into Cassie's face, much to Max's amusement.

'And I thought blushing brides were a myth!'

This whole thing is a myth, thought Cassie bitterly, but, aware of Julia's watchful eyes, she smiled serenely at her brother-in-law. 'Just an old-fashioned girl, that's me, Max.'

'Not many of them around,' said Nick with relish, and slid his arm round her waist, pulling her closer still. 'I thought I'd better snap her up before someone else did.'

'Wise move,' approved his brother, and Alice perched on the arm of the sofa, close to Cassie, to admire the ring.

'Are those real diamonds?' she asked, impressed.

'The very best,' Nick assured her, and dropped a kiss on Cassie's hair.

Alice giggled. 'You kiss Cassie an awful lot, Uncle Nick.'

'Not nearly enough,' he said, sighing so theatrically everyone laughed, and Julia held out her hand to Alice.

'Come on, darling. Bedtime. Kiss everyone good-night.'

Max put down his glass. 'I'll see you upstairs, Miss Seymour. How long have I got, Julia?'

'Ten minutes or so before we eat.'

'Right, you stay here. I'll see to the girls.' His eyes met Julia's with a look which made Cassie glance away hastily, feeling she'd trespassed.

'Right,' said Julia rather breathlessly, when Max had taken Alice off. 'More champagne?'

'Yes, please,' said Cassie recklessly.

Nick gave her a sardonic glance. 'Finding it hard going?'

'Just a bit.' She smiled reassuringly at Julia. 'Don't worry. I'll be good, I promise.'

Once they moved to the dining-room Cassie felt better, away from Nick's encircling arm. At the dining-table, with no possibility of physical contact with him, she was able to contribute quite naturally to a conversation which centred mainly on Nick's experiences in the Middle East and her own job at the bank. Max refused to talk about his own adventure in New Guinea, telling them to wait for the book he would write in due course.

'Where Julia's job is concerned perhaps you two will help me persuade her to resign and come with me to Cambridge,' he added, looking at Julia, who gave him a faint, enigmatic smile, but made no comment.

Cassie began to relax gradually as the evening wore on, but the ring drew her eyes like a magnet. She glanced up to find Nick watching her, and looked away, flushing. Ring-gazing might be a practice most newly engaged females indulged in, but she wasn't newly engaged, just pretending to be.

'Are you all right?' he said in an undertone, when they were alone for a moment after dinner.

She nodded. 'But I feel such a fraud.'

'It won't be long now,' he whispered, leaning close. 'Another hour and it will all be over.'

Which had such a ring of finality Cassie's spirits sank to a new low. 'Yes,' she agreed, depressed.

'Don't look like that,' said Nick urgently. 'You're

supposed to be on top of the world and in love, remember.'

Half of which was true enough, thought Cassie, then stifled a gasp as he took her in his arms and kissed her very thoroughly, only releasing her when a theatrical cough interrupted them.

'Alice was right,' said Max to his wife as he put down the coffee tray. 'Nick does kiss Cassie a lot.'

'Only natural,' said Julia, smiling.

Max nodded, and met her eyes. 'I used to be the same where you're concerned. I still am.'

There was a sudden, electric silence all four of them broke at once, the two men with hasty conversation, while Julia, scarlet to the roots of her hair, seized the coffee pot and Cassie leapt to distribute cups.

Afterwards Max and Julia sat together on the opposite sofa, not actually holding hands, but with something in their body language making the nature of their relationship very plain to their guests.

Thank goodness, thought Cassie. She would miss Julia and Emily. Alice too. But they would all be living happily ever after in Cambridge. Which might be Julia's heart's desire, but it was a whole lot more than Max deserved.

It was still fairly early when Cassie tugged on Nick's hand and stood up, bringing him to his feet with her.

'I've got work tomorrow. Time we were off,' she said, looking up at him with a smile designed to show this was just an excuse to be alone with him.

'Whatever you say,' he said promptly, with an answering gleam in his eyes.

'I'll just go upstairs and get my coat, and peep in on the girls.' Cassie ran upstairs, glad to have a moment to herself in the guest-room. She took time to tidy her hair and renew her lipstick before putting on her jacket. Afterwards she tiptoed into the room next door, pulled the covers over Emily and gently retrieved Alice's book from the foot of her bed. Cassie stood for a moment, looking at the flushed, sleeping faces. One evening of play-acting for Max's benefit had been such a small contribution to make to a happy future for Alice and Emily. She backed silently from the room and went along the landing to rejoin the others, but stopped dead at the head of the stairs as she saw Nick take Julia in his arms in the hall below. She turned tail and fled silently the way she'd come, this time locking herself in the bathroom until she'd achieved some semblance of calm. When she finally went down again Nick was waiting with Max and Julia in the hall.

He looked up with such a blatantly possessive smile Cassie could have murdered him. 'At last, darling. I was about to come and look for you.' He bent to kiss Julia's cheek. 'Goodnight and thank you for a great evening.'

'Thank *you*,' said Julia quietly.

'It was our pleasure.' Nick held out his hand to Max. 'Are you staying up in London long?'

'No, we go back to Chastlecombe in the morning. Julia wants to spend New Year's Eve with her parents. What are you doing?'

'There's a party at Cassie's place,' he said, sliding an arm round her waist. 'Right, then, let's be on our way.'

'There,' said Nick in the car later. 'That wasn't so bad, was it?'

'That's a matter of opinion.'

'I would have come away even earlier,' he informed her.

'Then why didn't you say so?' she demanded.

'I left it to you. But towards the end I could see Max was reaching the end of his tether.'

'You mean he's still suffering the after effects of his fever?'

'I suppose you could put it like that,' agreed Nick dryly. 'Anyone more clued up on the subject than you, Cassie, would have noticed he was burning to get Julia to bed.'

Which makes two of you, thought Cassie bitterly, and wrenched violently at the ring on her finger. She winced as it refused to budge over her knuckle.

'This ring. I can't get it off. My finger's throbbing like mad.'

'If it's that tight we'll have to get it cut off.'

'Where are we going to do that at *this* time of night?'

'Emergency department at the local hospital, I suppose. Let's see what we can do at your place first.'

When they arrived at the house Nick rushed Cassie into the kitchen and seized her hand. Under the fluorescent light the diamonds flashed on a visibly swollen finger.

'Give me your jacket,' he ordered, and flung it on a stool. 'Right, turn the cold water tap on and hold your finger under it as long as you can.' He picked up a coffee mug, filled it with ice from the freezer, then thrust her hand into it without ceremony. 'That should reduce the swelling.'

Cassie stared down at the slim brown fingers encircling her wrist, her vision obscured by sudden tears. She made no sound, keeping her head bowed, her face hidden by her hair, but Nick felt teardrops on his hand and jerked her head up, his face altering dramatically.

'Cassie, don't cry! We'll get the ring off somehow.'

'Just hand me a tissue,' she said thickly, sniffing hard. 'I'm not crying because my hand hurts.'

'Why, then?'

'Because the entire evening was such a horrible strain.' Cassie mopped her eyes with her free hand. 'I kept feeling Max was on to us. I was terrified it was going to blow up in our faces any minute.'

'You're wrong. Before we left he told me very emphatically he couldn't be more pleased. Remind me to give you an Oscar.' Nick drew her hand out of the ice. 'How is it now?'

'A bit better.' Cassie reached for the washing-up liquid, and squirted it liberally on her finger. Gritting her teeth, she began to turn the ring, the detergent acting as a lubricant as little by little she unscrewed the ring from her painful finger like a cap from a bottle. When it clattered to the draining board at last she let out the breath she'd been holding and handed the ring back to Nick. 'There!'

He thrust the ring into his breast pocket, then raised her hand to examine the reddened finger. 'How does it feel?'

'Sore. But I'll live.'

'I'm sorry, Cassie. Your hands are small. It never occurred to me the ring wouldn't fit.'

'It doesn't matter,' she said indifferently. 'I was only worried because the ring belonged to your mother.'

'An inspirational thought on my part—one look at that and Max knew I meant business.'

'*Believed* you meant business,' she corrected tartly, and suddenly she'd had enough. 'Could you go now, please? I'm tired.'

Nick moved closer. 'So this is goodbye, then, Cassie.'

'I suppose it is,' she agreed curtly.

'In that case—' He pulled her to him, bending his face close to hers. 'Kiss me goodbye and part friends, Cassie.'

'Friends?' she retorted scornfully, and Nick looked down into her eyes for a long, tense moment, then straightened and stepped back.

'So. I'm still the enemy,' he said wearily. 'All right, Cassie. Have it your way. It would have been easier for Julia if we *were* friends, but I doubt we'll all be together very much now Max is taking her to Cambridge.'

Always Julia! Cassie's chin lifted proudly. 'Good-night, Nick. See you around.'

He hesitated for a moment, then shrugged indifferently. 'Happy New Year, Cassie. Goodbye.'

This time when Nick left he closed the door behind him with quiet finality. Cassie stared at it in misery for a moment, then turned round like a sleepwalker and went back to the kitchen. Tea, she thought dimly. Maybe that would help. But after she'd made it and drunk it tea proved to be no cure for what ailed her, nor had she expected it to be.

Cassie wrestled with herself for a while, trying valiantly to hold back the tears, but at last, defeated, she laid her head on her arms on the table and sobbed her heart out.

'Cassie!' Polly catapulted into the kitchen, and threw an arm round her shoulders. 'What is it? Are you ill? Don't cry like that, please. *Jane,'* she yelled. 'Come here. Cassie's upset.'

Jane came running, and Cassie pulled herself together, assuring her friends there was nothing physically wrong.

'Ah!' Polly threw off her coat and sat down beside her, putting an arm round her shoulders. 'Then it's a man. Which one? The delightful Rupert or the sexy pirate?'

'Which do you think?' said Cassie thickly, and blew her nose on the tissues Jane provided.

'It's her sister's brother-in-law,' explained Polly.

'You're crying your heart out over *him*?' said Jane, mystified.

'You'd know why if you met him,' Polly assured her with relish. 'Anyway, Cass, I thought you were just having dinner with Julia. What did he do?'

'Nothing,' said Cassie bitterly, scrubbing at mascara smudges.

Jane and Polly exchanged a look over the bowed fair head.

'You're in love with him?' said Jane gently.

'I suppose so. Though if this is love you can keep it.' Cassie heaved in a shuddering sigh.

'But if he's your sister's brother-in-law you're bound to see him again,' said practical Jane.

'Not,' said Cassie malevolently, 'if I see him first.' She shook her head at the offer of more tea, coffee, wine, or anything else likely to help. 'No, thanks. Sorry about all the emoting.'

'Gosh, Cass, I've never seen you cry like that before,' said Polly with concern.

'You won't again, either, if I can help it. Men! Who needs them?'

Jane and Polly united on keeping Cassie out of the doldrums the next day by the simple expedient of keeping her too busy to mope. Polly was on the staff of a glossy magazine, Jane worked in the personnel department of a large department store, and normally they only met up with Cassie at home. But they appeared in time for

Cassie's lunch hour at the bank and chatted animatedly over a meal about their party, a perfect antidote for a dented heart. Their costumes were ready, and they checked their guest list and settled on how much food and wine was necessary.

The theme of their party was pantomime, and the three of them were appearing as a group. Dark-haired Jane, the tallest and slimmest, was cast as Prince Charming, blonde Polly the Fairy Godmother, and Cassie was bullied into the Cinderella role. Typecasting, she thought, resigned, but flatly refused any nonsense about a ballgown. Designer rags or nothing, she'd insisted, but gave way to Polly's plea to get her hair done in ringlets again.

By the time Cassie got home from the hairdresser later that evening it was late and the house was buzzing with pre-party excitement as half-dressed females dashed about, borrowing mascara and curling tongs, and squabbling about time in the bathroom.

'The food's arrived,' said Polly, as Cassie came in. 'Looks yummy, all those bits and pieces. But not very filling. I hope everyone eats something stodgy before they come.' She eyed Cassie's hair critically. 'Even better than before. You look great.'

'Wow, Cassie, that looks fabulous!' agreed Jane, rushing in. 'But the rest of you looks fragile. Eat something. Have some tea. Or milky coffee.'

'You sound like my mother,' said Cassie, accepting the sandwich Polly passed her, but she was touched. It was nothing new for the household to rally round when one of them suffered a setback in the romance department. But in the past she'd always been one of the comforters, never the comforted.

But this was New Year's Eve, Cassie told herself as she rushed through a swift bath. Time to put her troubles away and enjoy herself. When she was ready she eyed herself critically in the pier glass in her room. Polly, the clever one with a needle, had made her a skimpy outfit of thin pink lining cotton, slashed artistically here and there to make it look like rags, with a few smears of dust added for realism. It was cut a shade low at the neck and high on one thigh for Cassie's taste, but the result was perfect according to Polly, when she rushed up to hurry Cassie along. She grabbed needle and thread and put in a few stitches to make the dress fit more securely, then stood back to admire her handiwork.

'Wow—*very* sexy. Damn! Want to swap costumes?'

Cassie shook her head, laughing, as she eyed her friend's floating gauze and silver wand. 'Not a chance. You look gorgeous—like something off the Christmas tree.'

'I was afraid of that,' said Polly glumly, then brightened as music began thumping downstairs. 'I hope Meg and Hannah are having fun in their Alpine chalet—I bet they'll be mad as fire they missed all this. Put a move on, Cinderella, lots of people are here already. Let's be off to the ball.'

As they went downstairs roars of laughter greeted the awkward entry of a doe-eyed pantomime cow inhabited by two young men from Cassie's group at the bank. Laughter and catcalls greeted each new arrival as Red Riding Hood came mincing in with a large and hairy wolf, followed by a slender female Aladdin with a spectacularly well-built genie. Rupert, elegant as Robin Hood, was among the next to arrive, and Polly, furious with her Jack for coming as Little Red Riding Hood, promptly detached Rupert from Cassie and pulled him off to dance. Most of the men present were regular visitors to the house, and for the next couple of hours

Cassie was rarely allowed a minute to herself, but at last she detached herself from Dick Whittington and escaped with Jane and Polly into the kitchen.

'Time we passed out some of this food,' she panted, thrusting her tumbled ringlets out of the way. 'I don't fancy eating any of it for breakfast.'

Jane cast an eye at the clock. 'Not long to go, so let's feed them before we top up glasses ready for midnight.'

The food disappeared like lightning, and when the dancing began again Rupert seized Cassie before anyone else could get in first, pulled her close to a slower beat and gazed down into her eyes soulfully.

'You look so cute, Cassie,' he breathed in her ear.

Cute? 'Having a good time, Rupert?' she asked brightly.

'Fantastic,' he assured her. 'Especially now I've actually managed to get Cinderella to myself again. I only wish I was Prince Charming instead of Robin Hood.'

I wish you were, too, thought Cassie sadly, as the music changed to a fast, thumping beat, and space was cleared for the irrepressible Polly, who was gyrating wildly with the large, muscular genie, to the wrath of Jack, who'd changed his Red Riding Hood cloak and curls for jeans and T-shirt, and stood glowering from a corner, glass in hand.

A few minutes later Jane beckoned to Cassie urgently. 'Come *on.* It's nearly midnight—and don't even think of disappearing on the stroke of midnight, Cinders!'

Cassie laughed as all eyes turned towards the television in the corner of the big room to watch Big Ben strike the first chime of midnight in Westminster. Polly, to her surprise, gave her a kiss, looking flushed and very excited, then went off to join Jack. Glad to see Rupert was on the far side of the room, cornered by a very animated Snow White, Cassie would have given much to escape to her room and see in the New Year on her own. Then the doorbell rang, and she frowned, surprised, certain that everyone invited was already here. She went along the hall, opened the door a crack, then stared in utter amazement at the guest who'd come late to join the revels.

CHAPTER TWELVE

THE newcomer gave her a smile which flipped her heart over under her rags. Familiar black hair caught back into a false switch, a growth of black stubble along his jaw, Nick wore a gold ring in one ear and a full-sleeved white shirt open almost to his wide, buckled belt. He stood with long, black-clad legs apart, the deep cuffs of his tall leather boots turned over at the knee, one hand on the cutlass hanging from his belt as he gazed down into Cassie's stunned face.

'Crikey,' said someone behind her. 'It's Blackbeard the Pirate!'

There was a burst of laughter as Nick took a speechless Cassie by the hand to make a bow, then everyone turned back to the television screen and began chanting the countdown to midnight.

Cassie looked up into the familiar black-fringed blue eyes, all questions as to how and why Nick was here unimportant as he took her in his arms at the first, sonorous stroke of midnight.

'Happy New Year, Cinderella,' he said, and Cassie caught a glimpse of Polly's triumphant face across the room as the hubbub of congratulations and kisses broke out. Then Nick kissed her, and went on kissing her, despite howls and catcalls that were meant to break them apart.

When he released her at last Polly yelled, 'This is Julia's brother-in-law, everyone. Nick Seymour.'

'Brother-in-law?' hooted someone, and there was a

concerted roar of laughter, except from Rupert, who looked as if someone had just punched him in the stomach.

'I asked for something slow, Cinderella,' said Nick, when the music started up again. 'Will you dance with me?'

Since Nick usually ordered rather than asked, in Cassie's experience, she had an idea he was asking much more than that, but without hesitation she melted into his arms and he held her close. They moved together in silence, as much as it was possible to move at all in the crowded room, and after a while Nick manoeuvred Cassie gradually towards the door into the hall, drew her into the kitchen and closed the door.

'Have you come from another party?' she asked, suddenly shy now they were alone.

'No.' He gestured at his blatantly macho costume. 'All this is for you, Cassie.'

'You knew about the party, of course, but I didn't mention fancy dress,' she said breathlessly.

'Polly told me when she invited me, suggested I come as Prince Charming.' He leaned against the door, his eyes gleaming in a way which accelerated Cassie's heartbeat to the point where Nick could have heard it if the music hadn't been so loud. 'But I remembered something you once said.'

'Pirate king turned sober engineer,' she said, nodding.

'No. Not that. You told me that once upon a time you were turned on by my long hair and the earring and designer stubble. I couldn't grow my hair in time, but the beard is never a problem, and this earring clips on. I drew the line at ear-piercing again—even for you, Cassie.' He moved away from the door, and she backed instinctively. 'You can't run away from me here, darling.'

She swallowed. 'You said Polly invited you.'

'Yes. She seemed to think you might be glad if I came tonight. Are you?'

Cassie stared up at him, mesmerised by the glitter in his eyes. 'Yes.'

'Why?'

Suddenly she remembered why she shouldn't even be speaking to him, let alone admitting she was glad he'd come to the party. 'Because I'm an idiot,' she said bitterly.

'Is there any more wine left?' asked Jane, rushing in. 'Oh, sorry. Didn't mean to interrupt.'

'You're not interrupting anything,' Cassie said deliberately, opening the fridge.

'Why not?' her friend demanded, eyeing Nick belligerently. 'Talk sense into her, will you? She's been pining.'

Cassie handed Jane an armful of bottles, wanting to hit her over the head with one of them. 'I have not!'

'In actual fact,' said Nick quickly, 'would you think it rude if I steal Cassie off for a bit? After all,' he added, eyeing Cassie's costume, 'she should have vanished at midnight, anyway.'

'Great idea,' said Jane with enthusiasm, and rushed off again.

'I'm not going anywhere!' said Cassie fiercely, as Nick seized her hand.

'Just for an hour. I'll bring you back any time you say.'

'It's our *party*. I can't just leave in the middle of it.'

'Of course you can.' Nick hooked his thumbs in his

belt, eyeing her in challenge. 'Or I can act in character, sling you over my shoulder and carry you out. Choose!'

Cassie glared at him mutinously, but in the end put on the coat he fetched for her and went out to the car he'd double parked outside in the street.

'I should have said something to the others,' she muttered as he tossed the cutlass in the back seat.

'Unnecessary. They know I'm stealing you,' he added with relish.

'Where are we going?'

'Home.'

Cassie stared at his profile. 'Whose home?'

'Mine, of course. I do have one,' he added with sarcasm.

She sat back in her seat without argument, her mind a whirlpool of mixed emotions. Half of her was wild with delight just to be here with Nick. The other half couldn't forget the scene at Max's. Cassie's resolve hardened. Now was as good a time as any to tell him what she'd seen. Whether Julia had objected to the embrace or not was irrelevant. Nick had instigated it. And the scene she'd witnessed had kept her awake all night. Nick's dramatic appearance at the party had blotted it from her mind for a while, it was true, because she'd been so glad to see him. But now she was back in her right mind again.

Nick lived in Notting Hill, in a first-floor flat with high ceilings and tall windows. But Cassie had no attention to spare for her surroundings. When Nick took her coat and removed his own, Cassie suddenly felt embarrassed in her rags.

'Why are we here?' she demanded.

'To talk.' He led her to a sofa and gently pushed her down on it. 'Wait there for a moment. I shan't be long.'

He left the room, giving Cassie time to look round. It appealed to her strongly. As she looked round at Nick's possessions, with time to herself to think, she came to a decision. Tonight, at the party, Nick had demonstrated very publicly that he wanted her. In fact he'd made it clear from the moment they'd met again that he found her physically attractive. Something which had probably taken on a new dimension since their night at the farm—for her rarity value, if nothing else. So now was the perfect time to make a New Year resolution. Instead of hurling accusations at him she would do her utmost to make him forget Julia. Dominic Seymour's going to fall in love with me instead, decided Cassie.

It was some time before Nick returned. When he finally rejoined her he'd shaved off the stubble, removed the switch of hair, changed the boots for shoes and buttoned his dramatic shirt up a bit more, none of which did much to lessen the effect he had on his guest.

'Sorry to keep you waiting. What would you like to drink, Cassie?' he asked. 'I've got champagne, if you'd like it.'

'Thank you,' she said sedately. 'None of us at the house dared have more than a sip or two of wine in case the drink ran out too soon. But could I do something about my face first, please?'

Nick eyed the smears of dirt with a grin. 'All right, Cinders. Bathroom along the hall on the right.'

The face that greeted Cassie in Nick's bathroom mirror was very different from the one she'd seen in her own lately. The wan look had vanished, replaced with a glow whose provenance was only too obvious. She wiped the smears from her face carefully, gave up any idea of trying to do something to her hair, and, wishing she'd chosen the satin ballgown now instead of rags, went back to rejoin Nick.

Two lamps set on tables at either end of a deep, comfortable sofa gave the only light in the shadowy room, creating an intimacy which made Cassie's plan of campaign easier still. When Nick gave her a glass she smiled at him with a warmth which plainly surprised him.

'Happy New Year, Nick,' she said, raising her glass.

'Happy New Year,' he responded, and touched the glass to hers, holding her eyes with his as they drank. He held out his hand. 'Come and sit down. Are you warm enough like that?'

She nodded, and sat down beside him on the sofa, no longer caring that her rags revealed rather more of her person than was wise. When Nick took her hand in his and moved closer Cassie leaned against him pliantly, secretly triumphant when she heard him catch his breath.

'I thought you'd be fighting me tooth and nail at this point,' he said huskily.

'I should be,' she agreed. 'You could have warned me you were coming to the party.'

'Polly advised me not to.'

'Polly,' said Cassie dryly, 'has been very busy on my behalf.'

'For which I'm grateful. Though I gather she was the spokeswoman for the household,' Nick informed her, smoothing a finger over the back of her hand. 'She told me you were very unhappy, Cassie, which made me want to come rushing round to your place to ask why. Polly advised against it. She said the best idea was to provide myself with a Prince Charming costume and appear at the party on the stroke of midnight and carry you off.'

Cassie stared at him in astonishment, then began to

laugh. 'No wonder she looked so dumbfounded when the Pirate King arrived instead.'

'Can you honestly see me as Prince Charming, Cassie?' he demanded.

She smiled slowly. 'As it happens, I can. Though the pirate gear was infinitely more sexy.'

To her surprise Nick looked discomfited. 'It was a private joke just for you, Cassie, to soften you towards me. I tried to ring you but your phone was engaged all the time. Do those friends of yours ever stop talking on it?'

'Not much,' said Cassie, feeling better by the minute.

'Polly'd told me beforehand about the costume bit, and left a message on my machine to remind me. I wasn't too keen in the beginning, but when I spotted Rupert done up in tights as Robin Hood I was glad I'd made the effort.' Nick leaned closer. 'You make an irresistible Cinderella, Cassie Lovell.'

'I was told I looked cute,' she said demurely.

'Cute!'

Cassie felt suddenly breathless. 'You're still wearing the earring.'

'I remembered it turned you on in the past.' His grasp tightened. 'Does it still work?'

'You don't need it any more,' she said in a constricted voice, and turned her eyes up to his in such open invitation Nick's blazed and he pulled her into his arms.

'Cassie,' he groaned. 'Have you any idea how much I want you? I can't sleep for thinking of you in my arms that night.'

'Neither can I.'

Nick stared down into her eyes, breathing faster. 'Is that the truth?'

'Surely Polly told you that, as well as everything

else!' She hid her face against his shoulder. 'I've been so miserable since you walked out, Nick.'

'You mean since you sent me packing!'

Her head went up. 'You want an argument?'

'No,' he growled. 'I want to make love to you.'

'Then what are we waiting for?' She slid off his lap and stood up, holding out her arms.

Nick leapt to his feet and picked her up, and carried her swiftly to his bedroom. He sat down with her on the bed so suddenly they collapsed against the pillows, locked in each other's arms, kissing wildly. Nick sat up, stripping off his shirt as he looked down at the dishevelled ringlets and glowing face above the tattered dress, the gleam in his spectacular eyes accelerating Cassie's heartbeat. He pulled her upright, holding her against his bare chest with one hand while the other searched for the zip on her dress.

Cassie gave a breathless little laugh. 'I'm sewn into it. You'll have to cut me loose.'

Nick groaned impatiently. 'Will you want the dress again?'

She shook her head, then gasped as he tore the dress apart and threw the remnants on the floor, leaving her in the pearl satin teddy Julia had given her for Christmas.

Julia, thought Cassie, remembering her resolution. She pushed Nick away gently and stood beside the bed. He knelt, motionless, watching her every move as she slid lace-edged strips of satin from her shoulders very slowly, feeling triumph rise inside her as Nick's eyes dilated until they were darker than her own. She dropped the garment on the floor, stepped out of it and stood with hands behind her back, the heat in his eyes so fierce she felt it on her turbulent breasts like a burn.

Then Nick dived across the bed in a rugby tackle and

pulled her to lie beneath him, kissing her with such savage abandon Cassie forgot about her role as temptress as his hands and mouth caressed every part of her eager body, until at last they were joined in frenzied pursuit of the glory they experienced simultaneously, dark eyes locked with triumphant blue.

Cassie fell asleep at once. When she woke the first light of dawn was appearing through a crack in the curtains, illuminating the unfamiliar room. She turned her head on the pillow to find Nick watching her, and smiled into his eyes.

'Good morning,' he said, and reached out a hand to brush back a handful of hair from her face. 'Did you sleep well?'

She thought about it. 'I must have done. I've only just woken up.'

'I know. I've been watching you.'

'That's not fair!'

'All's fair in love and war, darling. And last night it was definitely love.'

'Was it?'

'How else would you describe it?' Nick moved closer and kissed her ear. 'What do you want right now?'

'A shower would be nice.'

'Whatever madam desires.' He slid out of bed, stretching his tall, tanned body, and laughed as Cassie hid her face in the pillow. 'Sorry. I'll get a dressing-gown.'

When he returned, wearing a short white towelling robe, he threw back the covers, ignoring Cassie's screech of protest, and carried her off to the bathroom to deposit her in the shower.

'Be careful, it gets hot quickly,' he warned, and gave her a towel. 'Wrap your hair in that. I don't possess a hairdryer.'

But when Cassie tried to draw the curtain he shed his robe and joined her, pulling her close as he began soaping her with caressing hands.

'Darling,' he said hoarsely, and turned off the water, spinning her round in his arms so he could kiss her. They towelled each other dry, then he picked her up and carried her back to bed, and it was very late on the first morning of the year before they lay quiet in each other's arms at last.

'Well?' he said softly. 'Am I still the enemy, Cassandra Lovell?'

'No.'

'So what am I, then?'

Good question, thought Cassie.

'I should make it clear,' Nick said with care, 'that I don't think of us as friends.'

She was in full agreement there. 'Relatives?' she enquired.

'Tricky, under the circumstances. Do you find it so hard to think of us as lovers?'

Not in the least. 'It's such an emotive sort of word,' Cassie said slowly. 'Not much used in the company I keep. Polly and Jane and the others have boyfriends, or refer to their "men".'

'How do you refer to me? If you ever do, that is.'

'As Julia's brother-in-law.'

Laughter rumbled in the chest Cassie was lying against. 'Sounds vaguely illegal somehow.'

'It's not illegal to lust after your sister-in-law,' she said softly.

He looked at her in silence for a moment, eyes narrowed, then got out of bed and pulled on his robe. 'Time we had that talk, I think. The nature of the beast being what it is, last night I forgot about talking in my indecent haste to make love to you.'

Cassie tensed. 'I'd like to talk. But there's a problem,' she told him.

'Just one?'

'One at a time, anyway.' She cast an eye at the heap of rags on the floor. 'I'm a bit short of clothes.'

'So you are. If you give me a moment to get dressed I'll remedy that.' Nick collected some clothes swiftly, and went off to the bathroom. After a while the outer door closed, and, puzzled, Cassie jumped out of bed to visit the bathroom herself. When she emerged from her second shower of the day she borrowed Nick's robe, rinsed her mouth out with something refreshing she found on his bathroom shelf, then used his hairbrush to restore some sort of order to her hair and found Nick watching her in the mirror.

'Your change of costume's on the bed, Cinderella. When you're dressed come to the kitchen. I'll make breakfast.'

Cassie eyed him uncertainly. The earring was gone, and something of their recent rapport with it. She went past him into the bedroom and stared in astonishment at the sight of her own familiar suitcase sitting on the newly made bed.

'I've just been out to the car. Your fairy godmother smuggled this out last night when I took you into your kitchen,' he informed her, and went out, leaving her alone to dress.

Polly had provided fresh underwear, sheer dark tights, boots, yellow sweater, and the suede jacket and skirt Cassie had splurged on in the sales, plus the basic requirements for teeth, hair and face. Fairy godmother indeed, thought Cassie as she dressed quickly. When she joined Nick in his kitchen, scents of freshly ground coffee reminded her that she'd eaten very little in the past twenty-four hours.

'That smells good,' she said brightly, as Nick waved her to one of the two chairs drawn up to the small table he'd laid for two.

'I've made toast, but I could rise to eggs in some form if you like,' he offered.

'Toast will be fine,' said Cassie, a sudden, loud rumble from her stomach giving the lie to her words.

Nick raised an eyebrow and put more bread to toast before he sat down. 'Will you pour?' he said formally.

Suddenly the funny side of the situation struck Cassie and she bit back a giggle. Less than an hour ago they'd been making mad, passionate love together. Now they were behaving like polite strangers.

'Are you going to share the joke?' he enquired.

She shook her head and poured the coffee. Afterwards, still in silence, she buttered toast and spread marmalade, then put down her knife with a clatter. 'All right, Nick, you obviously took exception to the word "lust",' she said bluntly.

'Not at all. I took exception to the word "sister-in-law" because I know you were referring to Julia—as usual.' He looked her in the eye. 'But since you've brought up the question of lust it seems a good time to say *I* thought I was making love to you. You, Cassie. No one else.'

She took the bull by the horns. 'You didn't say so at the time.'

Nick frowned. 'I thought I'd said quite a lot.'

She quelled a shiver at the thought of whispered erotic endearments which set her heart on fire. 'You said a lot of—well, encouraging things in the heat of the moment.

But for all I know you always do. In those circumstances,' she added, to make things perfectly clear.

'Whereas you never said a word,' he pointed out.

But Cassie had wanted to. Badly. 'I'm not up on the right things to say. I'm a beginner, remember.'

'But a very quick study,' he said softly. And suddenly the warmth was back in his eyes. 'I obviously didn't make myself plain.'

She remembered her plan, and smiled at him invitingly. 'Never mind. Next time, maybe?'

His eyes kindled, and he leaned towards her, then smothered a curse as the phone rang. He jumped up to get it, then handed it to Cassie. 'It's for you.'

'Cassie?' said Polly. 'Sorry to interrupt, but your mother just rang to wish you Happy New Year, and I didn't know what to say so I said you'd just slipped out for a moment.'

'Oh. Right. Thanks, Polly. See you later. All right if I ring home?' she asked Nick.

'Of course.'

Cassie wished her parents Happy New Year, told them to pass on her good wishes to the others, and was informed that Julia and Max had taken the girls for a walk and would probably ring her later.

Cassie explained rapidly to Nick, bolted the rest of her coffee, and asked if he'd mind driving her back to Shepherd's Bush.

'I do mind,' said Nick flatly. 'Ring Polly, tell her that all messages can be rerouted to this number until further notice.'

'Further notice?' she demanded, bristling.

'Yes.' He got up, leaning his hands on the table. 'Because I'm not letting you out of here until I know what's wrong. I honestly thought I'd convinced you last night—

and this morning—that I love you, Cassie. Is it so hard to believe?'

'Yes, it is,' she said bleakly. 'I saw you with Julia.'

He frowned. 'When?'

'I was upstairs on the landing when you took Julia in your arms.'

He ground his teeth in frustration. 'I might have known!' He came round the table to yank her to her feet. 'So,' he said, glaring down into her eyes. 'Let me get this straight. The moment you and Max were out of sight for ten seconds I snatched Julia in my arms for a spot of illicit passion. Is that what you're saying?'

'I know what I saw,' she said desperately.

'In which case why the hell did you let me make love to you last night?'

'Do you want the truth?'

'Probably not. But tell me anyway.'

Cassie looked up at him defiantly. 'I decided I'd try to break you of the habit.'

'What habit?'

'Wanting Julia. I thought I'd try to make you fall in love with me instead.'

The tension drained from Nick's face. 'Just so Julia could live happily ever after with Max?'

'No! Can't you leave Julia out of it for once?' she said angrily. 'I just wanted you to want *me*. Stupid, romantic idiot that I am—'

Nick caught her to him and kissed her into silence, one hand sliding into her hair to hold her still as he kissed her with hunger and relief and passion all rolled into one.

'It was the mistletoe,' he said unevenly, as he raised his head.

'Mistletoe?'

'While you were taking hours to put your coat on upstairs Max couldn't resist kissing Julia under the mistletoe, and afterwards, to my amazement, he pushed Julia towards me so I could do the same. The gesture was obviously more to do with olive branches than mistletoe, so I obligingly gave Julia's cheek a fleeting, chaste peck—with the full approval of her watching husband.'

'Oh,' said Cassie, exultation drowning any remorse.

'If,' went on Nick relentlessly, 'you'd mentioned it the same night we could have cleared it up a damned sight sooner.'

And saved her from the most miserable day of her life. Suddenly so happy she wanted to sing, Cassie grinned up at him provocatively. 'In which case you might never have turned up in that preposterous pirate gear.'

'Don't you believe it.' He smiled triumphantly. 'I had it all planned the minute I heard about your fancy dress party. I was determined to break down your defences once and for all, Cassandra Lovell.'

'You did,' she assured him, and reached up to bring his head down to hers so she could kiss him. 'Not that I had many from the moment you charged into the house hurling accusations at me about Alice.'

But Nick wasn't listening.

'What's the matter?' she asked, trying to read the look in his eyes.

'That's the first time you've kissed me of your own accord.'

'It won't be the last,' she assured him.

'Can I have that in writing?'

'I'll send a fax to your office if you like.'

Nick laughed and rubbed his cheek over her hair, then

eyed the uneaten toast on the table. 'After all that emotion I'm hungry. Let's have a proper breakfast.'

Cassie nodded with enthusiasm. 'I'll cook. What have you got?'

In a remarkably short time, despite Nick's insistence on kissing the cook every minute or so, they were eating scrambled eggs with smoked salmon, and drinking champagne.

'This feels very decadent,' said Cassie happily, as they sat side by side, as close as they could get.

'But great for special occasions. And not many occasions get more special than this,' said Nick, and pulled her on his lap to kiss her. Cassie responded with such fervour he groaned in frustration when the cellphone on the table rang again.

'Why, hello, Max,' he said, his eyebrows raised incredulously at Cassie. 'Happy New Year to you, too. Er, yes,' he added, trying not laugh, 'she is. I'll hand her over.'

'Cassie? I thought you must be there with Nick,' said Julia with satisfaction. 'Hope we didn't get you out of bed.'

'*Julia!*' said Cassie indignantly, then began to laugh as she realised Julia was very nearly right. 'Does that mean you and Max have only just got out of *your* bed?' she retaliated.

'Chance would be a fine thing,' retorted her sister. 'We've got a little alarm clock called Emily, remember. We just go to bed early instead.'

'Does that mean all's well now?'

'Very much so. Sometimes I pinch myself to believe it's all happening. How about you two?'

Cassie looked up into the blue eyes so close to hers. 'Julia wants to know if all's well with us.'

For answer Nick bent his head and kissed her, taking his time over it.

'Sorry about that, Julia,' said Cassie breathlessly, when she could.

'Was that little pause what I think it was?'

'Yes.'

'Thank goodness. *What* a relief. Just a minute.' Julia broke off for a moment to carry on a whispered conversation in the background. 'Right, Cassie,' she said after a moment. 'I just told Max we could stop pretending now.'

Cassie frowned. 'What do you mean?'

Julia gave an apologetic little cough. 'Now don't be cross, love, but Max and I knew from the first moment we laid eyes on each other on Christmas Day that nothing would keep us apart any more. Though it took a day or two for me to get back to—well, being really married again.'

Cassie gave Nick a speaking look. 'Then why the dickens were Nick and I supposed to pretend to be in love?'

'We thought you needed a push in the right direction. When I told Max you were convinced Nick was in love with me we cooked up the story of his lingering suspicions to get you together. And it worked, didn't it?'

'You actually mean you've been having a *game* with us?'

'But with the best of intentions,' Julia assured her.

'So all the time we were trying to bring you two together, you've been doing the same for us?' Suddenly Cassie began to laugh, and Julia joined in, and eventually Max took the phone from his wife to wish Cassie a Happy New Year. And this time Cassie was able to wish him the same with sincerity.

'Would you believe it?' she said to Nick afterwards, as they cleared up after the meal. 'We've all been involved in a right old pantomime.'

'A fairy story, not a pantomime,' Nick contradicted, a light in the blue eyes which brought Cassie into his arms like a homing bird. 'I flew home from Riyadh resigned to Christmas alone in a hotel,' he said against her hair. 'And look what happened instead!'

Later, that evening, when they were listening to music together on Nick's sofa, he turned her face up to his. 'Cassie, let's get serious.'

She looked at him apprehensively. 'What about, exactly?'

'We need to get a few things straightened out between us, once and for all. First of all, my darling, I love *you*, not Julia, nor any other woman in the known world. And second, I'll swear I'll never treat you like Piers did—'

'Oh, I know you won't do that,' she said promptly.

Nick's eyes narrowed. 'Does that mean you actually trust me at last?'

'As it happens, I do. Now, anyway. But quite apart from that I know you won't behave like Piers.'

'If you mean I won't leave you for another woman, you're right.'

Cassie gave a sudden, bubbling laugh. 'Piers didn't either. The love of his life wasn't a girl.'

'What?' He whistled incredulously. 'Oh, I see. That explains a lot!'

Cassie nodded. 'My experience with Piers put me right off men for a while, and Max was no help, either.'

Nick drew in a deep breath and held her tightly, as though determined to protect her from all future hurt. 'In which case it amazes me that you let me make love to you at the farm. Why did you, Cassie?'

'The moment you kissed me it just seemed so right for you to be the first,' she said simply. 'I love you, Dominic Seymour.'

He kissed her, and gave a deep, relishing sigh. 'I suppose in one way I've got cause to be grateful to Piers. Because of him I was your first lover. And I'm going to be the last too. Your one and only,' he added with emphasis. 'You agree?'

Cassie did, wholeheartedly, and demonstrated it in a way so satisfactory to them both there was no more conversation for some time.

'I suppose you realise,' said Nick later, 'that this means a big wedding, with Alice and Emily for bridesmaids and all your pals from Shepherd's Bush throwing rice and horseshoes, and so on.'

Cassie sat bolt upright in astonishment. *'What?'*

The blue eyes danced wickedly between the enviable fringe of lashes. 'Max rushed Julia into a Register Office, remember, with just a small reception at your parents' house. This time your mother will want the works.'

'How about what *I* want?' demanded Cassie.

'Don't you want to marry me?' demanded Nick.

'Of course I do, now you've mentioned it. More than anything in the world,' she added. 'But not just yet. Let's just savour our feelings privately for a while. The minute we mention "wedding" we'll be swamped in arrangements and invitations and all the rest of it. We won't have a moment's peace.'

Nick eyed her thoughtfully. 'Does this mean you want me to come calling for you at Shepherd's Bush like the others?'

'No, it doesn't. I thought I'd just move in here—if you want.'

'Are you mad? Of course I want.' He leapt to his feet. 'Let's go and collect your things right now, before you change your mind.'

Cassie giggled. 'At this time of night? I'm too comfortable right here. Besides, I won't change my mind. Ever.'

Nick sat down again and took her on his knee, pushing the tumbled hair back from her face. 'I won't either,' he assured her, in a tone which made her tremble inside.

'In that case,' she said, clearing her throat, 'could you have your mother's ring made bigger some time?'

He grinned, and took it out of his pocket to slide it easily on her finger. 'I already have!'